33 snowfish

33 snowfish

ADAM RAPP

CANDLEWICK PRESS
CAMBRIDGE, MASSACHUSETTS

The author wishes to thank his agent, Bill Reiss,
for his gentle persistence and his editor, Liz Bicknell,
for her unwavering fearlessness.

First edition 2003

"Hushabye Mountain" by Richard M. Sherman and Robert B. Sherman
copyright © 1968 (renewed) EMI Unart Catalog Inc.
All rights reserved. Used by permission of Warner Bros.
Publications U.S. Inc., Miami, FL 33014.

Library of Congress Cataloging-in-Publication Data

Rapp, Adam.
33 snowfish / Adam Rapp; Timothy Basil Ering, illustrator. — 1st ed.
p. cm.
Summary: A homeless boy, running from the police with a fifteen-year-old,
drug-addicted prostitute, her boyfriend who just killed his own parents,
and a baby, gets the chance to make a better life for himself.
ISBN 0-7636-1874-8
[1. Homeless persons — Fiction. 2. Child sexual abuse — Fiction.
3. Babies — Fiction. 4. Sick — Fiction. 5. Middle West — Fiction.]
I. Title: Thirty-three snowfish. II. Ering, Timothy B., ill. III. Title.
PZ7.R1765   Aae 2003
[Fic] — dc21 2002031156

2   4   6   8   10   9   7   5   3   1

Printed in the United States of America

This book was typeset in Perpetua.
The illustrations were done in ballpoint pen, pencil,
acrylic wash, and coffee on 2-ply bristol.

Candlewick Press
2067 Massachusetts Avenue
Cambridge, Massachusetts 02140

visit us at www.candlewick.com

"Then it was over. Over in the sense that he was gone and I knew that, see him again though I would, I would never again see him coming swift and secret to me in the woods dressed in sin like a gallant garment already blowing aside with the speed of his secret coming."

— Addie, from William Faulkner's *As I Lay Dying*

THE SKYLARK

Custis

On top of everything else, Boobie's got the clap. On Highway 53 he couldn't stop swallowing screams. It got so bad he had to pull over and get out of the car. When I checked on him he was backed up against a telephone pole pouring Gatorade down his pants like some kind of scientist.

Curl kept going, "What's he doin', Custis? What's he *doin'*?"

I guess he thought them vitamins and nutriments would cool that burning. The Gatorade was green like Martian blood. I never heard someone scream so loud in my life.

Curl's got the clap, too, but she quit crying after we changed to Highway 38. Her face went soft and dreamy all of a sudden. Them towns like Maple Park and Elburn and Cortland went by all quiet and spooky with their fields and cows and farm machines.

"Look at that big dumb cow," Curl kept saying. "And that one, too. Look at him. He's so big and dumb."

Curl says you get used to the clap after a while. She says living with that burning's like breaking in new shoes.

I'm in the front seat scouting pigs.

Pigs get crafty on the highway and you gotta concentrate. They go undercover and paint their cars and tint up their windows. On Interstate 80 a pig car might be red and it might be blue. I seen one once that was yellow like a banana. It's all about them big antennas. If it's got one coming off the trunk and it's a Impala or a Caprice Classic, you can bet your spending money it's a pig.

I got my gat in my pocket and my hand's on top of it just in case. It's been on top of my gat ever since we skated. It feels like my fingers is all grown into the trigger.

Curl's in the back seat trying to name the baby. She's got her new dress on. It's green with this big sunflower down the front and when she sleeps she keeps her hand on the stem like she picked it in a field. This rich man from Joliet gave her the dress. Them rich suckers is always coming off the Harrah's gambling boat walking all tall and supreme like they ain't never gonna have no pain.

4

The radio's broke so Curl keeps singing Pepsi-Cola commercials and making Pigmy feet on the window; that's when you press the side of your fist up against a steam blob. If you press it right it looks like a little Pigmy foot. You can make toes with the tip of your finger.

Whenever Curl's fiending for bazooka, she smokes Boobie's Basics, and whenever Boobie's tapped out she makes Pigmy feet.

She's been counting blackbirds, too. She thinks that if she counts enough of them it'll clean her bazooka habit. Sometimes she counts them even though they ain't in the sky. Her voice gets all wack and desperate like someone's chasing her with a stick.

This morning there was this whole flock of them flying south. It looked like a big black flag flapping around in the sky. Curl got so excited she pressed her face up against the window and smeared all her Pigmy feet. She said she counted forty-seven of them, but I only counted eighteen. She spent the rest of the morning looking for them blackbirds like they was gonna come back and ask her for her telephone number.

Since then I've only seen three more, and one of them suckers was smashed to the road. Boobie pulled the car over so he could study it. Even though it was smashed you could still see its face. It looked like it was screaming.

Curl ain't been eating none lately either. You used to always see her with a fish sandwich and some French fries. Curl's crazy about fish. You stick some meat in her face and she won't eat it, but if you show her a live fish she'll cut its head off, clean it, and cook that joint up like she's been starving for the longest.

She used to go fishing in Bolingbrook with Old Man Turpentine. Old Man Turpentine says the best fish east of the Mississippi swim in the Des Plaines River. Him and Curl would drop their lines right next to those niggers with the straw hats who drive up from Kankakee in their old broken-down cars. Skankakee niggers, I call them. Even though they got their own river all to themselves they still come up to Bolingbrook. Old Man Turpentine says all they talk about is how rotten and little the fish are down in Skankakee.

Curl uses this old bamboo pole she found under a bridge, and even though it's all warped and smells like foot fungus she catches carp and bullheads and cooks them up in the barbecue pits over at Renfro Park.

I ain't never fished with Curl, but Old Man Turpentine says she catches more fish than them niggers from Skankakee, and that's all they do.

Curl keeps promising Boobie that she's through with bazooka, but you know she's still fiending. You can see how them froggy eyes of hers slide to the left like she thinks she can smell it cooking somewhere, like she can picture it getting scraped out of the pot and trimmed up on the kitchen table. And you can see that yellow starting to crawl where her eyes is sliding, too. Naming the baby's the last thing on Curl's mind.

Boobie wants to name it, cuz you can't sell no baby that don't got no name. He wants to call it Eugene or James or some shit. One of them rich-sounding names from New Lennox or Frankfurt or the west side of Joliet.

I knew this kid from the west side of Joliet called Wallace Henry Walters. He lived on Western Avenue, and he had a pool in his backyard with two diving boards. He let me live in his tree house for a few days cuz I stole him a calculator from the RadioShack on Larkin. It was cool cuz it had this window and you could watch squirrels and shit. He said I could live there as long as I wanted, but then his pops — this big sucker who looked like a anchorman — caught me pissing in the bushes and called the police.

Wallace Henry Walters.

Rich people like a name like that.

If you ask me, the more names you use, the better chance you got of selling a baby. As long as it's got two eyes and all its fingers and it ain't no nigger. That's what I keep telling Curl, but she just shakes her head and sets them big froggy eyes on me and tells me I'm evil.

"We're lucky he ain't no nigger," I'll say. "We're lucky."

"You a evil boy, Custis," she'll say. "You evil like a priest on Monday."

Curl thinks I got evil in me cuz of Bob Motley — this fat man who used to own me. He was keeping me at his duplex over by the Rockdale water tower. I stayed in the room where Sergeant Dick used to sleep. Sergeant Dick was his dead pit bull, and you could see where he was trying to chew the door up. Sergeant Dick's room was cool cuz it was warm and I got to sleep on top of a real Sealy Posturepedic mattress. Even though it was on the floor and it smelled like dog spit, it was the first real mattress I slept on since I stayed at this halfway house in Lockport, and them mattresses was all skinny and wack.

In Sergeant Dick's room you didn't care about the pit bull smell so much cuz at least you was warm and them Rockdale vagrancy pigs wasn't gonna fuck with you.

Bob Motley found me at the mall when I was stealing half-Cokes from the food court. You can get pretty full on half-Cokes if you drink them fast enough. You can swallow air in between so it makes you feel fuller, too, but sometimes that gives you ass failure, so you can't swallow too much.

That day in the food court I wasn't wearing no kicks cuz I left them in that tree house on Western Avenue. This security guard tried chasing me but I hid behind them caramel corn ladies with the big fat stomachs.

"Hey, ladies," I said. "Let me mop your floor. I'll do it for free."

"How old are you?" they asked, smiling like big, happy dolphins.

"Old enough," I said.

"How old is old enough?" one of them replied.

I was like, "Eleven, twelve, thirteen. Twenty-seven."

They just thought I was cute and let me mop their floor. They didn't even notice my bare feet.

"What's your name?" the fattest one asked me.

I was like, "Ronald."

"Ronald what?"

"Ronald McDonald."

They laughed and laughed.

I stayed behind the counter and ate caramel corn while the water was filling up the mop bucket.

"Make sure you add some bleach to that water," one of them ladies said.

"Oh, I will," I promised. "I'll add some bleach."

When they wasn't looking I pissed in it. I bleached up that mop water real good.

As soon as that security guard took his cigarette break I skated to the food court and found a table by Sbarro and hid my feet under a copy of the *Daily Shopper*.

Bob Motley walked over to me all fat and slow with his beard and his sunglasses and his big hairy shoulders and gave me a slice of pepperoni pizza and pointed to the *Daily Shopper* and told me he'd buy me some new kicks if I took a ride with him.

"A ride where?" I asked.

"Just a ride."

I was like, "Cool."

He got me a pair of Pro Flyers with lightning on the sides and took me over to his house in Rockdale.

That's when he started owning me.

In the TV room at Bob Motley's there was this hole in the wall where he was always hiding shit. He called it the Dumdum Hole. He kept a bike chain and a paddle with nails in it and a pair of nunchucks and a Louisville Slugger baseball bat in there. The Dumdum Hole went through the entire wall, and when you peeled the newspaper away you could see the front yard. There wasn't much to look at but a rusty-ass barbecue grill and a bunch of weeds. I think he made the Dumdum Hole by pushing Lottery's head through the wall. Lottery was this seven-foot Indian who lived on a houseboat on the Illinois River. He used to fall down and have epileptic seizures a lot, but he was good at hearts and he didn't never fuck with you, and once in a while he even gave you some beef jerky to eat.

Bob Motley says he cured Lottery of them seizures when he made the Dumdum Hole. Lottery didn't never come by after that.

"Cleared that boy's head right up," I heard Bob Motley bragging to the rest of his crew one night. There was like eight of them suckers, and Bob Motley's duplex was like their headquarters.

Bob Motley had a PlayStation II and a Mitsubishi VCR and so many videos you couldn't even count them joints. He also had this big electric saw that he kept in the kitchen. He used it to slice up roast beef and Virginia honey-basted ham, and it would spit little meat boogies all over the place. He'd always make me clean it up, and whatever I missed the bugs got.

Bob Motley never really looked at me, and he yelled a lot, but he kept me fed and got me them Pro Flyers and sometimes when he was in a good mood he would even let me touch his pet iguana, Mercy. He got Mercy from this man from Minooka who owed him some money. He kept Mercy in a glass box next to the electric saw. Mercy was cool cuz she would flick her tongue on your hand.

After a while Bob Motley started calling me Boy, which was cool cuz before that he'd just call me Hey.

Before I skated me and Bob Motley made like four films together. The best one was called *Girl Eats Boy,* where Bob Motley puts this black pillowcase over his head and pretends like he's cutting me with the electric saw. Then he grinds up my legs in a hamburger maker and feeds me to this little girl who lives under the kitchen sink.

Making *Girl Eats Boy* was pretty cool cuz I got to scream a lot.

The little girl's name was Wendy Sue. She was like seven or some shit. I think she belonged to one of Bob Motley's boys, but I ain't sure. Wendy Sue stayed with us for a whole weekend. It was cool cuz she slept with me on the Sealy Posturepedic mattress in Sergeant Dick's room. One night I pulled her shirt up and stared at her body. She didn't even know it cuz she was sleeping.

After that weekend I never seen Wendy Sue again. You got to wonder what happens to a kid like that.

Bob Motley said he was going to get *Girl Eats Boy*

put on the Internet. He said you can make crazy bank with them computer films.

Making movies is fun, but watching movies is boring. When him and his boys would play hearts, Bob Motley used to make me watch this movie called *Chitty Chitty Bang Bang*. *Chitty Chitty Bang Bang* is like the most boringest movie ever made. It stars this man called Dick Van Dick, which is a pretty wack name if you ask me. My favorite part of the movie is when Dick Van Dick saves all these kids from a evil child-catcher. He sings this pretty crisp song called "Hushabye Mountain." These two rich kids are hiding under this toy maker's shop, and they get lured into this candy truck and wind up at the baron's castle where the child-catcher lives, and they meet up with all these other kids who are hiding under the castle, and some of them was already *in* the castle, but they escaped and they kept talking all frantic about how they had to pretend that they was like dolls so they wouldn't get caught and that's when Dick Van Dick comes and sings the song.

One day when I was watching *Chitty Chitty Bang Bang* I went into Bob Motley's room to use the toilet, cuz the one in the basement was busted. His boys had skated and Bob Motley was asleep on his waterbed. He was making this face like he was in a car crash, and whenever he made that face he wouldn't wake up for nothing. For some reason I opened his closet. There was all types of stuff in there, like boots and boxes of porno magazines and a electric guitar. There was a gas mask in there, too, and when I put it on it made me feel alive and dead at the same time.

There was a shoebox that had DEATH TO ALL WHO MEDDLE on it. I opened it and there was my gat, just waiting for me to take it. It was the blackest thing I ever seen, and as soon as I touched it I got a boner and I knew I wouldn't never be able to let it go. I'll bet Bob Motley still don't know I took it. He probably had like a whole collection of them little guns.

It only fires twenty-twos and it ain't no bigger than a hand and the trigger's busted, but a gat's a gat, and that's that.

It's only got four bullets in it, but four's better than none.

Once, I heard this old, blind sucker at Renfro Park say that if you shoot the right four or five people you'll grow a new life. He's one of them Vietnam vets who lives in a refrigerator box. He said he missed the ones he was supposed to hit and hit the ones he was supposed to miss. He says that that's how come his life never grew back right. That's probably how come he lives in a refrigerator box in Renfro Park.

I ain't shot nobody yet, but I would. You never know who's gonna creep up behind you.

Anyway, when it comes to names, that Wallace Henry Walters kid's got one of them fancy ones. You can almost *sing* that shit.

A baby without a name just ain't marketable.

Even cars get good names. Horizons and Neons and shit like that.

Besides, the baby is Boobie's little brother, and Boobie don't want that non-name on his head always reminding him of what he done back home. It's like naming the baby makes shit new again.

Even a non-name will get behind your mind. That's how come ghosts always call out a name when they're floating through walls and shit — they know it'll get stuck way in the back of your head where the brain can get a scream caught in it.

Even though it ain't hers, Curl thinks we'll get at least five hundred for the baby, but she don't really know. She's too busy fiending.

"Five hundred," she'll say. "Five hundred solid, right Boobie?"

I keep telling her you can't just open a catalog and look up some numbers — it's a *baby*. And some people might think there's something wrong with him, cuz he's got this little seam down the middle of his forehead.

At first Curl wanted to take him by Sidekick's. Sidekick is this man who used to make movies with Bob Motley. He was tall and skinny and he laughed so much you thought his teeth was going to fall out and shit. His favorite thing to do was to chill in parking lots with his big, long arm hanging over the door to his El Camino. He mostly just hunts little kids. Sometimes he hunts kids who are littler than me. He finds them lost at the mall or stranded down by the Rockdale bus station.

Once Sidekick found this little half-nigger called Ulysses crying under the big sign at Arthur Treacher's Fish & Chips. Sidekick gave him a pack of Fleer baseball cards and Ulysses got right in his El Camino like there was about skeighty-eight more packs in the back seat or some shit. Sidekick always keeps Tootsie Rolls and Wrigley's Spearmint gum in his pockets, too.

After Sidekick got Ulysses to get in his El Camino he made him put his seatbelt on and gave him a 1999 Susan B. Anthony silver dollar.

I know all that cuz Ulysses showed me the silver dollar. Susan B. Anthony looks like a man; like her name should be *Dave* or some shit. Ulysses used to come over to Bob Motley's duplex with Sidekick for the Thursday hearts game. They would stick him in Sergeant Dick's room with me, and we would watch *Chitty Chitty Bang Bang* and he would tell me all the wack shit Sidekick was doing to him.

Ulysses was only like seven or eight and he talked with a stutter and he had this little purple spot on his neck that looked like a flower. He was a dirty-ass little half-nigger, too — a lot dirtier than me. And he wasn't dirty in no dusty way, he was dirty in a *skanky* way. Like he was always shitting his pants and sitting down in it and stuff like that. That's probably why his parents didn't want him no more.

Once I asked him where he was from.

I was like, "Where you from, Ulysses?"

He just looked at me funny and went, "The United States of America."

After a while, Ulysses just disappeared. Whenever I'd ask Sidekick about him he would just say he wasn't "useful" no more, or how he kept getting "smaller and smaller" till he just "faded away." Then him and Bob Motley would laugh their stupid laughs and trim up some hurricane on the kitchen table.

On Thursdays Sidekick would bring other kids to Bob Motley's, too. It was like you would see them for a while, but then one day you wouldn't no more.

That's how come I'd never get into Sidekick's El Camino with him — cuz it was like if you got in it and the door closed you would start to disappear. That's how you wind up on the back of one of them milk cartons you see at the Econofoods in Coal City.

I ain't no fucking milk carton kid, I'll tell you that right now.

When we got to Sidekick's crib with the baby the windows was all boarded up and the El Camino was gone and there was this big black X painted on the door.

Sidekick lived in Bolingbrook over by Old Man Turpentine's Fun Shop. That sucker always had the pigs or some bill collector looking for him. He's probably been in thirty different states by now. Or maybe he's down in Mexico eating a taco or some shit?

I skated from Bob Motley's duplex after I found out

he was gonna put me in this snuff film. One day when him and his crew thought I was sleeping I heard them talking about shooting the film and how much money they could make and how many hookers they could get and how much hurricane they could buy.

I was in the kitchen sneaking some Folger's instant coffee.

"We could use your boy," one of them was saying to Bob Motley. "One minute he's doin' his thing, and the next thing Mr. Snuffleupagus pays him a visit and it's all over. He won't know the difference."

Bob Motley was like, "I guess we could, I guess we could."

After his crew left I had to hide in the basement till Bob Motley drank his two bottles of Mad Dog and fell asleep in his big corduroy chair.

When I came up from the basement I peeled away the newspaper, pushed the Louisville Slugger aside, crawled through the Dumdum Hole, and ran all the way through Rockdale.

That night I slept under a bread truck in the parking lot of the Dominick's on Jefferson Street in Joliet. When I woke up I had a burn on my arm that still bleeds when I lean on it wrong. Curl thinks it's a evil spirit that got freed when I left Bob Motley, but I just think it's from the bread truck.

At the Fun Shop Bob Motley was always telling Old Man Turpentine how he's gonna cut off my hands when he finds me. Old Man Turpentine don't never say nothing, though, cuz I used to clean his floor for him.

I knew Boobie wasn't going to let Bob Motley touch me, though, cuz whenever some sucker started messing with me Boobie would just walk up to him and use his fist or a stick or something he'd find on the street. Sometimes he'd even just stand there and stare at them with his black eyes. He did it to a nigger in Lockport once and the nigger started running away all frantic like his house was burning down and shit. Boobie's protective like that with Curl, too.

But the thing about Boobie is that most of the time you don't *never* know what's on his mind. No one does. That's cuz he don't never hardly talk. He mostly just *does* shit. And when he ain't *doing* shit he's thinking real quiet or he's drawing pictures in this special book he carries around with him.

At first I thought he was writing scary stories, but Curl looked in the book and she said it was just a bunch of drawings.

One page's got a picture of a old man with no mouth.

Another one's got a picture of a horse getting attacked by a hawk.

Curl said he names them pictures, too, but even though she's smarter than most people, she can't read too good.

I learned how to read a little in the basement of this Catholic church in Streator. This nun called Sister Pat teached me the alphabet song and had me putting letters together and building them syllable parts. Sister Pat had all of these sores on her mouth, and she was always blessing me and making them crisscross signs with her hands.

Sometimes if I would get letters fixed together right to build them words, she would try to kiss me on my face, so I started calling her Sister Blister.

I'd go, "Cool out, Sister Blister," or some shit like that, and then she'd get pissed and make me sit in the holy chair and sing this wack church song about God and the love he's got for children and blind people in Maryland or Jerusalem or Jahozifatz or some place.

And sometimes Sister Blister would make me hold the Jesus picture and sit in the holy chair and do thirty-threes. A thirty-three is when you count to thirty-three. It's supposed to make shit slow down. Sometimes it worked, but I'd usually fake it and be like, "Oh, I feel much better," just so she'd stop sweating me.

It's funny, cuz that picture of Jesus makes him look like one of them old homeless suckers you see shitting in the bushes at Renfro Park. He don't look like no miracle maker or no Son of God, I'll tell you that.

I only went to them spelling classes for a couple weeks, cuz that Streator church basement was cold and this other nun called Sister Blop or some shit started yelling at me after I got caught pissing on the floor in the boys' bathroom. I only did that cuz one of them retarded kids stuck a fan in the toilet and I didn't want to piss on it and get electrified.

They wasn't going to let me come back, but Sister Blister bowed her head and practically frenched them other nuns' fat asses so they let me stay. Sister Blop and this other nun with a kangaroo face called Sister Cordelia wouldn't go for it at first cuz they said I had too much devil in me, but Sister Blister kept telling them how I was *special* and they finally gave in.

But I left after a few days anyway, cuz when people start calling you *special* you know they're just trying to change you into something you ain't.

I think Sister Blister was trying to turn me into a retard, cuz she used to always make me sit with them. I'd be at the lunch table and I'd look around at all these retards and they would be staring at me like I *was* the devil. Just cuz maybe I was taking their fruit cups or stuffing French fries in my pockets or some harmless shit like that.

Every one of them retard kids got them mouths that don't never close and them little bald eyes that look like they was pressed too close together.

I *know* I would've started turning into a retard if I didn't skate from that Streator church basement. Cuz when you hang around certain types of people for a long time you start to *look* like them and shit. That's how come dogs start looking like their masters.

I knew this man who lived on a park bench and after a while he started *looking* like the park bench. He even started turning green, too.

But even though I skated from that Streator church

20

basement, Sister Blister teached me enough to read street signs and cereal boxes if them letters is big enough. I can even read them sex books in Old Man Turpentine's Fun Shop if I go slow and use my finger.

If I had enough time, I'd look in Boobie's book.

But I'd do it in private, cuz he'd jack you up if he caught you.

Boobie don't let *nobody* touch that book.

It's been almost a day since we skated. Boobie won't take none of them big toll roads like Interstate 80 or Highway 55. Curl says he's smart cuz that's the first place the five-oh starts looking.

So I just keep scouting pigs, and Curl's got her birds to count.

She's like, "Custis, you see any?" and I'm like, "There ain't none to see," and she's like, "Yes there is, you just have to look better!"

When someone's got a bazooka habit it's like the most boringest shit you'll ever see, I swear.

This morning Boobie stuck this Abraham Lincoln–looking sucker in the face for calling us white trash. All we wanted was some water from his hose. It wasn't like we was gonna wash the Skylark. That man came out all waving his arms and calling the Joliet pigs on his cell phone. And the Joliet pigs will come a lot quicker than the pigs in Rockdale. They'll bust you a lot quicker, too, cuz they get paid more money.

Before he could get them numbers dialed, Boobie snatched his cell phone and stuck that man square in the eye. He stuck him good, too.

That man's eye swolled up so fast he had to sit in his bushes for a minute. After he stopped bleeding Boobie made him give us some money and this fancy metal pen from his pocket. But he smashed up that cell phone. He didn't want them cell phone pigs tracking us.

So now Boobie uses that pen to draw his pictures.

Even though he ain't but seventeen, Boobie's bigger than most men. He's definitely bigger than Bob Motley. He ain't fatter but he's taller. He's bigger than all of Bob Motley's boys, too. And he's already got whiskers.

Me and Boobie was making our crib in the woods till we skated. We had this tent with a dome and sleeping bags and pots and pans and everything.

The woods wasn't in Rockdale or Joliet. They wasn't nowhere really. No one goes out there no more, cuz they found some woman under a tree with her head torn off.

Boobie's parents kicked him out after he tried to set their house on fire. They had one of them fancy Joliet cribs by the Inwood Golf Course.

In the tent we had us about twenty-five extension cords hooked up to a paper company on the other side of the woods. We had a radio and a camping lamp and a double-burner stovetop that Boobie stole from the Costco in Crest Hill.

At night we would build fires and eat barbecued beans and watch the lightning bugs do somersaults.

Curl started living with us a few weeks later. You could hear her coming through the woods. She was calling out Boobie's name the way kids call for their moms when they get lost at the mall.

When we found her she was sitting under a tree with a bag of groceries. She was crying and her makeup was all smeared and she was wearing this rabbit-skin coat and a pair of bowling shoes stuffed with newspapers cuz they was like four sizes too big.

No one knows how old Curl really is. For some reason it's this big mystery. All I know is she was born on Christmas, but she likes to tell people she's a Pisces and that she was born at the end of February so she'll get more presents.

I know she was born on Christmas cuz she carries this old wrinkled birthday card in her pocket from when she was like three. It says:

> *Happy Birthday to my baby girl.*
> *Mary Christmas.*
> *Love,*
> *Mom.*

Curl don't know I know about that. Sometimes when she thinks she's alone she takes the card out and rubs her thumb on it. She hides that birthday card the same way you hide birthmarks.

She smokes Boobie's Basics like she's about thirty-two. Old Man Turpentine says she's really only fifteen, and he knows most things.

When we found her in the woods she was so desperate for bazooka she asked me if I was packing any and she didn't even know my name.

I wouldn't do that shit if you paid me. Old Man Turpentine says that bazooka makes your stomach disappear. I think it's true cuz earlier when we stopped in this Wisconsin town called Footville, just off of Highway 213, we opened the hood of the Skylark and fried a box of fish sticks on the engine and Curl wouldn't touch them. She just kept pushing them away like they was poison. Usually she'd eat half the box.

That day she came out to the woods we was glad she had them groceries. They was mostly Ding Dongs and Nutty Bars and packets of Lipton Cup-a-Soup and shit, but it was cool cuz we had something besides them barbecued beans.

Curl used to live with her Aunty Frisco. They stayed in Bolingbrook above Old Man Turpentine's Fun Shop.

Curl's Aunty Frisco's a cripple and has to use a wheelchair. She's a speed freak, too, and she's got Parkinglot Syndrome — that shit that makes your hands shake like they're electric.

Curl told me that Muhammad Ali's got that disease, too, and he was the greatest boxer who ever lived. She said you can get that shit anytime in your life, that it don't matter who you are. I probably already got it.

Sometimes I just start shaking for no reason. And sometimes I get these big-ass migration headaches that make me go blind and fall asleep and wake up in other places. It ain't no fun waking up somewhere else, I'll tell you that.

Aunty Frisco's the one who got Curl to trick. She stopped getting that hospital money when they found out she was speeding all the time. After that these old low-water suckers in brown suits started hanging around in the Fun Shop, and one by one they would disappear through the back door and head up the stairs.

At first they made so much money Aunty Frisco bought herself a new wheelchair with a motor in it. You could hear that thing revving all the way from the street.

Aunty Frisco didn't let Curl have no money, though — that's how come Curl started tricking on her own. Down in the Fun Shop them lines started getting smaller and smaller. Sometimes Curl would meet her tricks in Old Man Turpentine's back room. Curl says he was always looking out for her.

After Curl moved in with me and Boobie things started getting kind of nice, like we was in a real crib, with walls and food and bodies moving through it and light shining off of them bodies. Even though it was only a tent in the woods and there wasn't no real walls, it was still like that.

Sometimes I'd wake up and watch Curl's and Boobie's shadows moving. Then I'd close my eyes and listen to their voices groaning all hot and slow.

Sometimes the three of us would lay together just to stay warm. They'd let me in the middle cuz I'm the smallest. Sometimes Curl would even comb my hair and try braiding it. Even though I ain't no girl I'd let her do it cuz it's long, and she'd tell me stories about her tricks and that voice would get behind your mind the way a song can.

We had to quit cooking in the tent cuz Boobie almost burnt it down. He's got this freaky thing with fire. Sometimes he'll light a match and watch the flame drop all the way to his fingers. It don't even faze him.

Then one day the radio stopped working. And two weeks later all of that other homicidal shit happened with Boobie and his parents. And now we're just in Boobie's pops's spray-painted Skylark, scouting pigs and raiding Dumpsters.

So now I'm in it for the long run.

All three of us is.

Boobie made us make a symbolic pledge.

I didn't know what that meant but Curl said it was important.

We stopped the car on this gravel road in this town called Creston. Boobie made each of us close our eyes and fall backwards. First Curl and Boobie caught me, and then me and Boobie caught Curl. It wasn't easy catching Boobie cuz he's so big, but we did it. Afterwards we touched tongues and put some ants in a marshmallow and ate it.

Curl says pledges are good cuz they give you reasons to do shit.

I guess things ain't so wack, really.

As long as Curl finds some birds to count.

As long as them highway pigs don't bust us and the baby keeps quiet, there ain't no sense in complaining.

CURL

The thing about babies is they're always grabbing at your tits. This one's all over mine like they have Strawberry Quik inside. Baby hands are tiny but they're strong, and they know right where to grab. And always when you're looking out the window or watching the road slinking by; always when you're not paying no attention to them.

And when you're counting birds to keep busy those baby fingers are like little hot spiders crawling on you.

I was blowing in his face earlier, just to get him to stop crying because Boobie was looking at me in the rearview mirror with all those powers in his eyes. The minute you stop blowing the baby starts squeaking like Styrofoam. And that makes that itch come and you scratch it but that doesn't help much so you look for some birds to count but there isn't anything in the sky but that dirty metal color.

Those birds were there this morning.

Forty-seven blackbirds flying like a big smile in the sky.

I'm in the back seat with the TV and Custis is in the front looking for the police. Custis has his little skinny arms tucked in his shirt because he says it's cold, but I'm so hot it's like the sun's burning in me.

We found the TV in a Dumpster back in Rockdale. Boobie kicked out the glass and gutted it and me and Custis stuffed it with newspapers. It's perfect for the baby because if someone looks in through the window they just think it's some old Magnavox we bought from one of those garage sales on Theodore Street.

Even though it's only been two days it feels like we've been in the Skylark for forever. Boobie drives and pumps the gas and leads the Dumpster diving. When he sees something he likes he lifts Custis over the edge and tells him what to pick. You can find some pretty good stuff in a Dumpster. I found an old-fashioned typewriter once. I didn't ever use it, but I found it and took it home and put it in my closet. Some of the junky Dumpsters have rats, but they only jump at you if you corner them.

Before we left I made a hundred and fifty dollars tricking the trumpet player at Arlo's Blues Lounge. Arlo's is down in Belleville. It took like twelve hours for me and Boobie to get down there. The Greyhound bus was full of all these big sad women with dirty children. Thank God Boobie went with me because I would've been bored crazy. All of those little sleepy towns like Chenoa and Buffalo Hart and Farmersville just kept stretching south, and the further south we got the sleepier they were.

Practically every person on the Greyhound was wearing a St. Louis Cardinals baseball hat. When I got off the bus my legs were so thick and sandy I almost fell down.

It wasn't too bad once me and Boobie got settled. We stayed in a Red Roof Inn and had continental breakfast, which was pretty decent, with Krispy Kreme donuts and granola cereal with dates.

The next night when I left with the trumpet player Boobie was standing next to the jukebox and warning me with his eyes.

"No bazooka," I could feel his eyes saying to me. "None of that, Curl."

Besides that hundred and fifty dollars that old trumpet player didn't have crap in his pockets but some chump change and a box of Chiclets. Old Man Turpentine's the one who set me up with him.

"He'll be good to you, Curl," he kept telling me. "You do right by him and he'll be real good to you."

I didn't even have to do nothing but bend down and blow zeros on his stomach while he masturbated himself. Old men are funny like that.

Before we left Belleville me and Boobie ate Arby's roast beef sandwiches, and then it was back on the bus and all the way home to Rockdale. Those sad little towns were still there with their silos and grain elevators and fields with nothing in them but black dirt and pop cans. We drove by this one grassy field that had so many cows it was like they had plans to do stuff.

After we get up into the middle of Wisconsin we're going to use my Belleville money to get a motel. I could think of twenty other things to do with that money right now. At least twenty.

Sometimes it gets so hot in the back seat you have to roll the window down. But the baby doesn't like the wind coming through the crack. And when the baby cries it'll just about drive you crazy, because that little voice of his starts squeaking and it's like the TV came back to life and got stuck on a bad channel.

To tell you the truth, the baby isn't too smart. Sometimes when you say something to him he doesn't act like he hears you too good, but I think that's because of that little cleft down the middle of his forehead. It looks like he fell off the highchair before his brain bones were finished joining.

He has some cute little eyes, though. So blue it's like they aren't even blue. It's more like they're violet.

My Aunty Frisco said this old actress named Elizabeth Taylor has violet eyes and she's one of the richest people in the world.

Rich people will pay good money for some violet eyes.

Sometimes Boobie will take his lighter and flick it next to the baby's face so he can see the flame dancing in his eye. It's not like Boobie's trying to burn the baby or nothing like that; it's more like there's something in the flame that only Boobie knows and when it's dancing in the baby's eye the secret from the flame comes out purer.

Boobie's always got fire on his mind. My Aunty Frisco used to say that a man who has a strong relationship with fire is capable of historical love, because the flames keep the passion flowing in the smaller parts of the soul.

That's how I met Boobie — because of fire.

I was at the Knights of Columbus Speedway talking to some of them Rockdale paper-mill hooligans and I saw this tall, strong-looking boy standing all alone in front of a trash can. He didn't look like none of the locals because his shoes weren't junky. There was a fire burning in the trash can and he was staring at it so hard it was like he was talking to it with his mind. The fire didn't make sense because it was the middle of August. It was so hot even the mosquitoes looked tired.

I had no idea where he came from. It was like the dark of the night had imagined him there.

I got curious so I walked over and stood on the other side of the fire. I tried getting his attention by leaning real nice, because if you lean right just about any boy will look at you. And that's when I was pretty because things were good and my arms were clean. That's when my eyes were big and shiny. But no matter how many different leans I tried Boobie wouldn't look back, so I threw a rock at him. And that's when he did one of the most cold-blooded things I've ever seen: He just caught that rock and stuck it in his pocket like it was a quarter. And he was staring at that fire the whole time.

Just when I was about to go back over to those paper mill hooligans Boobie pointed at me. And he had this look on his face like he knew what I wanted the whole time.

We sat down next to that fire and listened to the tires squealing on the Speedway, and the fire was dancing off his face and moths were tumbling in the Speedway lights and you could see how something was howling inside him, and the next thing I know he's holding my hand and I'm touching his T-shirt and telling him all this stuff about myself.

Normally I wouldn't talk to no stranger like that, I don't care how fine he is or how much money he's got. But it was like those words inside me were being pulled out by the fire, and Boobie's hand on mine made the pulling part feel okay.

I told him about how I wasn't in school and how I liked to fish and how when I was a baby I had a ringworm infection in my foot and how I used to have this pair of white ice-skates and when the water froze I could do backwards figure eights on the pond in the Cedarwood Apartments and how I would watch the Chicago Cubs baseball games on WGN Channel Nine with my Aunty Frisco and how I used to want to grow up to be a play-by-play announcer but how that ended after this man called Harry Caray died from drinking too much Budweiser.

Boobie didn't even have to ask me any questions. It was all just coming out of me like water. I felt nervous and safe at the same time. I even started laughing for a minute, like I was crazy.

After the midget races stopped we fell asleep under the grandstand. Boobie wrapped me in his arms and blew on my eyelashes and everything felt warm, like when you have a laugh caught in your stomach. Because that's when things were clean and my arms were pretty. That's when my eyes were rounder than quarters.

As I faded off I could hear those Rockdale papermill boys walking across the gravel and calling out my name, going, "Curl . . . Curly Curl . . ." But their voices just sounded like some rain when your eyes are closed and you're sitting next to the kitchen window.

That night I dreamed of a huge snowstorm. It was a blizzard and the snow was piled up higher than all the houses. Then the sun came out burning like a big yellow planet of fire and all the snow melted and the Des Plaines River started boiling and there was this giant flood and everyone around me was sinking and screaming and swimming after their houses. But for some reason I wasn't scared. I was cleaner than the water and my eyes were big and shiny. Even though the flood was drowning everyone and the fish were getting cooked, I was safe. I was just floating and floating. I was floating so well it was like I *was* the water.

When I woke up it was the middle of the night and the crickets were humming and the moths were still tumbling and the moon was so big you could practically see the bones in its face.

Boobie's arms were all wrapped around me.

I've never felt safer in my life.

I don't think Boobie had no place to stay that night. I think that was the first time his parents kicked him out.

Boobie didn't say nothing that whole time under the grandstand. At first I thought he didn't have a voice. He just looked and nodded, looked and nodded. And sometimes he would half-smile, and every so often you could see his teeth when that half-smile got stretched a little.

I don't mind him not talking so much because you can hear his voice in your heart; the same way you can hear a song in your head even if there isn't a radio playing; the same way you can hear those blackbirds flying when they're not in the sky.

Getting used to Boobie not talking is like getting used to a cat that won't let you pet it. Or like when you have an itch but you don't have anything to scratch it with. After a while you just *picture* petting that cat or scratching that itch so you don't get too sad. Because if you get too sad that itch just gets bigger and then you don't feel clean anymore and those red streaks start crawling up your arm.

Sometimes I'll imagine Boobie and me talking about our future, like about buying some furniture or making a little garden with tomatoes and cauliflowers. Other times I'll just picture us talking about nothing, like the way wind and trees talk.

That silence can get to you sometimes, though, because it's not like his mind is bad. He's always drawing pictures in that book of his, so you know he has certain thoughts. Even when he says those little words like *stop* and *follow* it helps because at least you hear his voice. But he says those words the way you say them to a dog or a chicken. And then, just like that, there's that silence about him again.

Like clouds and a little bit of rain. Clouds and a little bit of rain.

He talks to me with his eyes mostly because of his powers. He has more black in his eye than a pit bull. My Aunty Frisco used to say that pit bulls aren't born out of a normal litter. She said that those dogs jump straight up out of the Devil World.

Once I saw Boobie stare one down. We were in the parking lot of the White Hen Pantry in Elwood. The pit bull was black and brown and he was just sitting there by the door waiting for his master, no leash or nothing. They locked eyes and Boobie stood so still it looked like he was carved out of some wood. Then something gave and that pit bull started crying for its master.

Most of the time eyes can say more than words, anyway. Eyes can tell you more about an itch, that's for sure—how it grows and how it knows. Nasty little itch. Eyes will tell you.

Back in Rockdale if me and Boobie and Custis were walking down the street together Boobie would stay about five feet behind us. Me and Custis would be talking about what we'd done that day, like how we stole some ketchup from the Burger King, or begged quarters from them clean-cut, suit-wearing college boys at the car dealership, and we would laugh and look back at Boobie and he'd be smiling at us.

Things were pretty cold-blooded back in Rockdale.

That's when my arms were so pretty I could hold them up to the light and see the veins curling all clean and smooth like little blue branches.

Custis looks up to Boobie like he's his daddy. Nasty little Custis. I swear, that hooligan would lay down on broken glass if Boobie told him to. I guess Boobie and Custis have one of those special friendships that young boys get sometimes. Something stronger than blood brothers.

I do like Custis, though. Even though he's a racist and he curses all the time and he doesn't know how to wash himself. It's not like he's mean or stupid. He told me about them spelling nuns trying to make him retarded, mixing him up with all them slow children. I've

37

seen Custis do smart stuff. He steals Boobie's Basics with the quickness. He'll walk by the cash register and throw a light bulb over his shoulder so it breaks in the aisle. Then when the checkout girl jumps he'll grab two packs of Basics and a box of Nerds, stuff it all in down his pants, and turn around and help sweep up the mess.

I'm always fixing Custis's clothes, too. His sneakers aren't ever tied right and he doesn't tuck his shirts in for nothing. My Aunty Frisco used to say that if your shirt isn't tucked you'll have to shovel coal, and I know Custis isn't capable of that. He'd probably be smaller than the shovel.

And he gets those migraine headaches a lot. Sometimes they're so strong he falls asleep and wakes up somewhere else.

I gave him one of my scarves to tie his leg down in case he knows one's coming. He keeps it wrapped around his leg like he got shot in the knee.

Once Custis passed out in front of the Rockdale train station and woke up on the back of a Greyhound on its way to Orlando, Florida. He says when those migraines come the only thing that helps is if he floats his hand in warm water. He usually pisses his pants but it makes the pain go away. I've had to give him one of my thongs to wear about four times. Most normal boys would fall out of a thong like a rock in a sock, but Custis is hardly developed yet. He still has that bald little boy package.

The other thing about Custis is that no one knows where he came from. It's like he crawled out of a rabbit hole. Or like someone drew him on a piece of paper and, *poof,* there he was, walking around Rockdale like a little lost cartoon. Once in a while he'll talk about this lady called Big Tiny. He does it when he sleeps. He talks about feeding the birds and staying off the curb and holding Big Tiny's hand and stuff.

Once I asked him who Big Tiny was and he just shrugged and said she was this old Rockdale lady he used to know who fell out of a window when she was trying to move a piano.

Old Man Turpentine says that Big Tiny was Custis's mom and that they didn't own a piano and that she had this little beard on her chin and that she committed suicide by eating her shaving mirror. Who knows what the truth is? I guess everybody's got some kind of story.

Custis is good with the baby, though. Thank God because I get tired of those little fingers crawling on me. Nasty little spider hands. Sometimes Custis even sings him this song called "Hushabye Mountain."

It goes:

A gentle breeze from Hushabye Mountain
Softly blows o'er Lullaby Bay
It fills the sails of boats that are waiting
Waiting to sail your worries away

It isn't far to Hushabye Mountain
And your boat waits down by the key
The winds of night so softly are sighing
Soon they will fly your troubles to sea

So close your eyes on Hushabye Mountain
Wave goodbye to cares of the day
Watch your boat from Hushabye Mountain
Sail far away from Lullaby Bay

The baby makes this face like he's glad when Custis sings that song.

At certain angles the baby looks like this old bus driver back on Theodore Street called Marshall Rose. Marshall Rose was always staring at you like he wanted to put hot sauce on you and eat you for dinner.

I would've done him if he didn't fart so much. Every time you got on the bus he was letting them fly. You couldn't get the windows cracked fast enough.

When you got off the bus Marshall Rose was always reaching out for you, too. And he would lock the middle doors so you couldn't get off without walking by him. I had to cut him with my keys once because he wouldn't let go of my wrist.

That's when my arms were still pretty and my eyes were big and deep.

I don't mind taking someone out back and putting a smile on his face if he's got something thick in his billfold. But when some hole-in-the-wall bus driver starts farting like that you can forget it. I put up with enough.

Like I said before, the thing I got going with Boobie goes beyond arms and legs and the skin on a hand. When me and Boobie do it, it's different. Because it's slow and quiet and it makes me cry. And no one's ever done me *that* cold-blooded before. My job is one thing and my heart is another. Tricking's like being a waitress or sacking groceries. It puts money in your purse. And when that money gets thick, things are usually okay. And you don't have to answer to no one if you don't have a pimp and I don't have one and I don't plan on tricking for one, either.

Most pimps wind up either knocking your teeth out or stealing all your money. You have to go solo if you want to get ahead in any real way.

Tricking's better than living in one of those Rockdale juvy hotels, that's for sure. In those Rockdale juvy hotels all they do is steal your clothes and burn you with cigarettes. And the supervisors who run them don't ever let you out if you don't have parents. And they feed you less and less so you don't ever get to grow up right, and for the rest of your life you just wind up being mostly a kid.

Those Rockdale juvy hotel supervisors know that stuff, too. It's not like they're trying to *help* you.

When I turn sixteen I'll probably start working a club like this one on the east side of Joliet called Harmony.

It's late hours and it kills the peaches in your cheeks, but the money's solid. I know some girls who bring home two hundred a night doing this thing called lap dancing. All you have to do is rub up against some college boy for a minute while he sits in a chair. You wear high heels and some booty floss and that's it. It's easy work. From what I hear you just walk around and when you start to feel someone's eyes on you — like one of them nervous suburban boys from Lewis University or the College of St. Francis — you offer him a dance. It costs him twenty dollars and he usually pulls the money right out of his pocket. The cool thing is that by law he's not allowed to touch you. But he wants to, that's for sure. And the longer he stays the more he pays.

Harmony has these big security guards, too, just in case one of those college boys gets out of hand.

My girl Dee lap danced at Harmony for a while. She made so much money she moved to Crown Point, Indiana, and started taking these correspondence courses so she could get a degree in administrative office management. I haven't heard from Dee in the longest but I'll bet she's doing real good.

I would lap dance just to make some profits because there's always the future to plan. Once me and Boobie and Custis get settled, we're all going to marry each other.

My Aunty Frisco used to say that if you don't have a priest or a judge or a ship captain you can still marry someone by jumping over a broom. That would be cold-blooded, all three of us jumping the broom like that. I'll get a white dress with some lace on it, and I know Custis will pick me a sunflower.

That's a ways off yet, though.

That's a long ways off.

Yesterday in this town called North Caledonia I saw Boobie's picture in the paper. Custis read some of it to me. He had to use his finger and he couldn't get all the bigger words right, but part of it said that the Joliet police are hunting Boobie for what he did to his parents. It also said that Boobie's real name is Darrin Flowers. Custis is scared but I keep telling him that the police don't have anything on him. They don't have anything on me, either.

It was smart of Boobie to disguise the car, though. He used about eight bottles of black spray paint that Custis stole from the True Value hardware store in Lockport.

Boobie got mad because I got lifted from all the paint fumes, but it wasn't like I was trying to. I just got what I could get from the air.

Boobie stole a pair of license plates from the parking lot at Mercury Cinemas, too. He scratched one of the letters off so the highway police can't track them. Now the Skylark looks like it got burped out of a volcano.

So the baby keeps grabbing at my tits and Boobie expects me to name him something that rich people would like.

I keep telling Boobie that rich people are just going to come up with one of their own names anyways. That's the thing about rich people: They have so much money they can buy their own rules. That's how politics work. If you got enough money you can win elections and stuff.

But I have enough to worry about. Like those blackbirds are all flying south and my arms keep itching and if I don't turn another trick we're going to run out of money.

Boobie's not crazy about me working right now but he knows it's the only way we'll get by.

Sometimes when things go quiet in the car and all you can hear is the four of us breathing, I get to thinking about my Aunty Frisco.

Before I moved in with Boobie and Custis she started throwing her china at me because I wouldn't come home at night. And after she broke her whole collection and didn't have anything else to throw she started locking her lungs until she would faint and fall out of her power chair. And the day before I left she took the broom and rolled over to me and tried to sweep under my feet, and if that happens you'll catch a curse so bad that no one will ever want to marry you. So I *had* to leave after that.

I can still see her all stuffed in her power chair, angry about the Cubs losing, shaking and speed-fiending and locking her lungs and cursing at those social workers who used to come and check up on us.

Sometimes I don't know how I got mixed up with Boobie. I mean, I love him and I love Custis, too, even though he's dirty and foolish and a nasty little hooligan most of the time. I guess I'm just afraid of what's going to happen. Because you can't run forever. There's only so much pavement that the road makers lay down. After a while, the highway quits going north and it just turns into the sky. And you can't go anywhere in the sky unless you have a plane or some kind of rocket.

My Aunty Frisco used to say that if you walk through a wheat field on the first day of May you will meet your fate.

In Bolingbrook there's nothing but parking lots and little short buildings, but on the first day of May, I went to the Jewel and bought some Chex cereal because it has wheat in it and I went behind the Fun Shop and spread it on the ground and sat on top of it all day. That's when things were clean and my arms were pretty. That's when my eyes were so big you could draw them.

Some birds came and tried to eat that Chex cereal, and I heard a fire truck go by, but other than that nothing special happened. I just sat there, waiting.

And when the sun went down and things started getting too private inside I got Old Man Turpentine to drive me to the Speedway, and that's where I saw Boobie staring at that fire.

So maybe that wheat field stuff's legit?

And now I'm going eighty in Boobie's dad's Skylark, looking for blackbirds and trying to name the baby.

There were forty-seven of them this morning. Forty-seven blackbirds flying like a big smile in the sky.

I think Charles is a good name.

Charles is good, and so is Marcus.

Later I'll change his diaper and feed him bananas and milk and hold him till he falls asleep. As long as he keeps those spider hands off of me I'll be okay. As long as the sun doesn't start burning in me too bad.

I don't know if I could sell my little brother. But then again I've never had one so I couldn't tell you for sure.

I guess Boobie has to do what he has to do.

BOOBIE

Custis

Boobie busted me watching him in Aladdin's Castle at the Joliet Mall. I'd just skated from Bob Motley's cuz of that film they wanted to put me in and I knew him and his crew would be hunting me.

You can always hide good in the Aladdin's Castle cuz of the Grand Prix game. If you're small like me you can squeeze under the steering wheel.

I was begging tokens from this rich nigger kid called Cato, and Boobie comes walking in all long and dark and restless with the money jangling in his pockets and them black eyes and that flowing hair and his one fingernail that he colors. I ain't never seen no colored finger-nail on no man like that before. I couldn't help but look. Once I watched this panther at the Brookfield Zoo in Chicago. This man called Jimmyjack took about ten of us there from the halfway house in Lockport. That panther was from a jungle in Africa and he was pacing in his cage, back and forth, back and forth. I almost had to stop looking cuz I started getting this feeling that he was gonna freeze me with the mirrors in his eyes. When the zoo lady fed it, it opened its mouth and you could see how pointy his teeth was. For some reason, Boobie's black fingernail was like that, too.

I turned back to Cato, who was jacking up Glass Joe in Punchout II, and I was like, "C'mon, Cato, lemme get a token," just to get my mind off of Boobie, and Cato was all, "Come on, yo, wait till my game's up!" but something inside me made me look at Boobie again.

Then all them video game sounds just sort of went quiet and my brain got all cold and for a second I thought I was gonna get one of them migration headaches.

All I remember is that when Boobie turned and walked out of Aladdin's Castle it felt like something inside me was gonna bust; like one of my lung bubbles was gonna pop or some shit.

I followed Boobie through the food court and out into the parking lot. It was so boiling outside you could feel the heat coming off the cars like they was breathing. Boobie passed all them cars and started walking down the street. I know he knowed I was following him, too, cuz he turned back and seen me.

He walked all the way past Five Corners and made that soft right onto Gaylord Drive and kept on going past the Crest Hill water tower. When he got to Rosalie's Roller-skating Rink he turned right on the noname gravel road and went into Crazy Lou's woods.

You ain't even supposed to go near them woods cuz Crazy Lou has all these Doberman pincher dogs; like skeighty-eight of them suckers. Bob Motley said Crazy Lou's a Marine who owns them woods all to himself and that he spends all his time shooting his rifle at birds and squirrels and all these cats that he farms.

That's pretty messed up if you think about it: farming cats like that just so you can hunt them. I ain't trying to say that I like cats, cuz them animals is greedy and nasty if you ask me; I'm just saying farming something just so you can hunt it don't seem right.

When we got into Crazy Lou's woods there was all these NO TRESPASSING signs nailed to the trees. Boobie was laying on the ground with his arms spread wide. It looked like he was sleeping. We was pretty deep in, so the sun wasn't coming through too crisp and the little bit of sky you could see looked all dark and bruised.

I stood over Boobie for a minute and then I started poking him with a stick. When I told Curl about that, she said it was smart cuz it's supposed to be bad luck to use your hand when you try to wake somebody. She says you're supposed to use a stick or some water.

First I poked him in the side and then I poked him in the leg and then I poked him in the hair cuz it looked all shiny and I wanted to see it move. And when it moved it felt like something *inside* me was moving, too, I ain't kidding.

I was like, "Hey . . . hey, kid. . . ."

Then out of nowhere, Boobie reached up and grabbed my hand and put it right on his hair. He kept his eyes closed when he did that, too, like he could see what I was doing with his *ears*. Then he guided my hand over his hair so I could *feel* how shiny it was, and that shit felt shinier than most things, I tell you that.

Boobie moved my hand up and down on his hair for like a minute. I don't think I breathed once the whole time.

Then he got up off the ground and he waved at me to follow him some more and I was like, "Cool," cuz I wasn't staying noplace noways.

On the way out of Crazy Lou's woods I started telling Boobie how I got busted the night before sleeping in the organ loft at St. Raymond's Cathedral and how this evil priest with jackknife eyebrows splashed holy water on me and chased me out, going, "He will feast on the depraved!" and shit like that.

Then when we got back onto Gaylord Drive I told Boobie how you can teach your body to sleep standing up if you practice enough; how all you got to do is find a good corner to lean up against — one that hopefully ain't been pissed in too many times — and how you just let your weight relax into it, and about how you should put some garbage down in case you fall but how after a while your body gets them muscle senses up and you *don't* fall.

And I told Boobie about how I used to sleepstand over in this corner at the Knights of Columbus Speedway, but how sometimes it was tricky cuz once them races start it gets too noisy cuz of how them tire screams sound like cats getting fucked.

And I told Boobie how I slept under that bread truck after I ran through Bob Motley's Dumdum Hole, and I showed him the burn on my arm and how it was all scabby and skanked.

And then once we got past Cedarwood Apartments I went quiet and Boobie just stopped and stood there for a minute and looked up at the sky, which was so black it was like God burnt it and shit, like the whole west side of Joliet was missing in that burn, like everything disappeared but the two of us.

Then we walked up Gael Drive and past the Day-n-Night, and the mosquitoes was dropping from the street lights all greedy and fat and Boobie waved to me to keep following him and I was like, "Cool," and then that dark sky started filling with stars and a little skinny piece of the moon and we was about to make a right on Black Road when Boobie spoke for the first time. His voice had some serious deep-freeze in it.

He asked me who my parents was and who I belonged to and if I had any money on me and shit like that.

First I emptied my pockets, but all that came out was some fuzz and a piece of candy corn.

Since Bob Motley didn't own me no more I told him how I didn't belong to nobody and how I was just trying to make my way, and then when I tried to tell him how I couldn't go back to that halfway house in Lockport cuz of how I got caught stealing money out of Jimmyjack's wallet, I started throwing up brown stuff. I think it was cuz of how my stomach was all messed up from eating Kleenex and ketchup and A.1. Steak Sauce.

Then after I spit all the brown junk out of my mouth he took my hand and held it and it felt like I was falling out of a tree, but falling without ever landing, and we didn't say nothing else and we was just walking on Black Road and watching the cars go by. And some of them cars was honking all crazy at us and calling us faggits cuz of how Boobie was holding my hand, but that didn't matter.

When we got to the highway there was a baseball game going and them outfield lights was like big flying saucers in the sky. You could hear some sucker announcing the batters and the crowd cheering and that ugly metal sound the bat makes when it hits the ball.

Just when we got past the baseball game some tall kid with a crew cut and a tattoo on his hand came walking toward us out of nowhere calling us the homo express.

He was like, "Well, if it isn't the Homo Express," and when he tried to trip me Boobie busted him square in the throat.

That tall kid had to sit down and cough into his fist for like two minutes.

We got his shirt and his shoes and about twelve bucks from his wallet.

After that we left him on the side of the highway and just kept walking.

That's when I knew Boobie was cool.

That's when I knew he would protect me.

Curl

Custis and me were dancing the night Boobie showed up with the baby. I'd been promising Custis that I'd teach him because he'd get so jealous every time he saw me and Old Man Turpentine dancing in back of the Fun Shop. He'd shuffle up to me all low and sideways with those desperate eyes, going, "C'mon, Curl, teach me to dance, you know you promised."

So there we were, outside the tent, dancing to Britney Spears, and Boobie's coming through the woods with a baby in his arms. The night was behind him like a big dark thing you can't see.

Custis was like, "Who's that?"

And Boobie shifted the baby in his arms and went, "My little brother."

"What's his name?" Custis asked, but Boobie just shook his head.

The General Electric radio was the only thing that let you know you weren't dreaming. It was either Britney or Pink or that little skinny bitch who can outsing all of them. There was so much blood on Boobie's shirt you could smell the metal in it, and it wasn't coming from the baby, because the baby was cleaner than a Christmas card.

The baby was making those Styrofoam sounds and Boobie was just standing there with his blackberry eyes looking scared and sad and that made me and Custis scared and sad, too, because we'd never seen Boobie like that before. It wasn't sad like tears are sad. It was sad like the weather is sad when you think it's spring but then one of those cold rains comes.

I got that small feeling that gets inside you when some badness is about to happen.

Custis started shaking because he hadn't eaten anything all day except for this stick he kept dipping in some Hellmann's mustard. And I had to sit down on the ground because my arms were itching so bad it was like ants were running on them.

I couldn't tell you what Boobie did to his parents. All I know is that there was blood on his shirt that night and according to the *North Caledonia Daily Register* Mr. and Mrs. Elliot Flowers are dead.

Boobie

THE OTEL MOTEL

USTIS

Last night we slept at the otel Motel. The otel Motel is
in this place called Little Chicago, Wisconsin. There ain't
nothing there but lakes and hills and big hairy-looking
trees. In the check-in office there was this man talking
about how he killed him a five-point buck. He was wearing a G.I. Joe jumpsuit and this orange hat with flaps.
That hat of his was so orange it looked like it would
have vitamin C in the flaps or some shit. I ain't never
heard of no five-point buck before. I kept imagining a
moose with a bunch of silverware on its head.

There was like skeighty-eight trucks in the parking lot. Strapped to the top of one of them was a dead deer. It might have been that five-point buck that that man was bragging about in the check-in office. Its eye was open and it was staring at me like it wanted to say something.

We stayed in room 4 and it was about the best place I've stayed in ever. The ceiling was kind of low but there was this pretty crisp wallpaper with fish on it. The bathroom was nice, too. There was these little soaps and shampoos and mouthwash and the towels smelled like them fancy department-store towels at the Joliet Mall. Even the toilet paper had little patterns on it.

The air conditioner was so powerful that when I held my hand over the blowhole it almost froze my fingers. It was getting cold outside so we didn't really need it, but me and Curl stuck it on anyway just cuz we could.

After the room got nice and cool, Curl fed the baby and gave him a bath. You could hear the water sprinkling and the baby splashing and Curl keeping his hands off of her titties, going, "Quit! Quit you!"

Later Curl and Boobie went to tip the vending machines and I left the room to go hunt change in the parking lot. I made sure the baby was sleeping before I skated. I even put a washcloth under his head and folded it up like a pillow.

It felt good just to walk around. I was weaving between all the trucks and checking the doors to see if they was open, cuz sometimes suckers will leave their toll money in one of them drink holders next to the panic brake and shit.

There was about skeighty-eight different license plates in that parking lot: Wisconsin, Illinois, Michigan, Ohio, Iowa, Missouri, Tennessee, and a bunch of others, too.

The truck with the dead deer was gone. For some reason I missed it. I couldn't stop imagining it riding down the highway with its neck all flopping around.

Way in the back of the parking lot there was this big-ass Winnebago fun home. It was white with a blue stripe, and it looked like if you went inside of it you wouldn't have to come back out for like ten years.

The only truck that was open was this old, rusty-ass Ford Ranger. When I looked inside all I could see was a box of Kleenex and some of them yellow and green deodorant trees hanging from the rearview mirror.

It was getting kind of cold out, but the sun was blasting down and it felt warm on my neck. For some reason I opened the door to the Ford Ranger and slid into the front seat. I found three dimes and a penny in the glove compartment. I also found this picture of a man holding a dead deer. He was lifting the deer up by its neck and smiling like he just won the Illinois Lotto and shit. The deer looked pretty bored.

I couldn't stop thinking about that other deer I seen

in the parking lot and how its eye was all open even though it was dead. You gotta wonder if animals go anywhere after they get killed. Like their souls and shit.

Back in that Streator church basement Sister Blister was always talking about the shape of your soul. She'd be like, "Your soul's not in very good shape, Custis. Not in good shape at all."

I wonder what the shape of that deer's soul is like. I bet it's all wack and infested cuz of the woods. There's probably like skeighty-eight flies buzzing around it.

I stuffed the picture down my pants and got out of the truck.

Back in the room there was this little kid sitting on the end of the bed. He was like six or seven or some shit and he had this Milwaukee Brewers baseball cap pulled down over his ears and he was wearing this puffy red coat that was too big and he was sitting on his hands and kind of rocking back and forth like he was about to piss himself.

He wasn't wearing no pants and his legs was all cold and wack-looking, like they would break if you bent them too hard. He was so short his feet wasn't even touching the floor.

His underwears was green with white checkers.

I closed the door and was like, "Who the fuck are you?"

He went, "Bruce."

"Bruce who?"

"Bruce Maloney."

I was like, "Whatchu doin' in here, Bruce Maloney?"

"Waitin'."

"Waitin' for what?"

"This man."

I was like, "What man?"

"Reggie."

"Oh."

I knew it was Boobie, cuz that's the name he uses when he's trying to be sneaky.

"Where'd he go?" I asked.

Bruce was like, "I dunno."

I pulled the curtains back and looked out at the parking lot. I could hear Bruce's tennis shoes squeaking.

I went, "Where'd you meet him?"

"We were playin' Ninja Destroyer in the game room. He just left with the TV. He said there was a dog in it."

"A *dog?*"

"A golden retriever puppy. He wouldn't let me pet it, though, cuz it was sick."

I was like, "You got any money?"

He went, "Nu-uh."

"You don't got no quarters?"

"No."

"Yes you do."

"I got a Junior."

I was like, "You got a *who?*"

"It's in my pocket, but *you* gotta get it."

I was like, "Why do I gotta get it?"

"Cuz my hands are tied."

He tried to show me his hands, but he was sitting on them.

I went into one of the pockets of his puffy red coat and pulled out this little clear plastic case that had a baseball card in it. There was this nigger's face on the card and he had these big white smiley teeth that looked like they was painted that way. It said "Ken Griffey Jr." at the bottom of the card.

Then he went, "I'll let you touch it if you untie me."

I was like, "I'm touchin' it right now."

Then he said, "I mean the card, not the plastic. The shiny part. You gotta open the case with a penny."

Then he tried lifting his knees, and I could see how his kicks didn't have no laces in them and how his ankles was tied to the bottom of the bed frame with the laces.

He was like, "I got a gun, too."

I went, "You got a gat, and I piss nickels."

"It's in my other pocket," he said. "Look."

Then I went into the other pocket of his puffy red coat and pulled out this wack little plastic gun that had a light bulb on the end of it. When I pulled the trigger it lit up like a Christmas tree and in this stupid-ass robot voice it went, "You are completely surrounded. Come out with your hands up!"

He was like, "You want it?"

I went, "That shit is wack, kid," and put it back in

his pocket. "You wanna see a real gat, I'll show you a real gat."

Then I unsnapped the big pocket on the side of my pants and pulled it out.

"See there?" I said, putting it on his cheek. "This is some real shit."

I popped it open and showed him the bullets and then I spun it in my hand Wild-West style and put it back in my pocket.

Bruce's legs was sort of shaking. I started pacing a little cuz his knees was wiggling and it was making me feel funny.

For some reason Bruce went, "Bet I could hypmotize you. Make you do the macaroni dance."

I was like, "What the fuck is the macaroni dance?"

He went, "Untie me and I'll show you. I hypmotize Bluster all the time and he does the macaroni dance."

"Who's Bluster?"

"My German shepherd. He eats potato salad and burps in the bed."

For some reason, picturing his dog eating some potato salad was making me hungry, so I was like, "You got any food?"

"That man already took it. I had two boxes of Hot Tamales and a purple gobstopper. I could get more if you let me go."

I went, "Get more from where?"

"The Winnebago."

I was like, "That fun home is yours?"

"Yep."

Then I looked out the window again and there it was in the back of the lot, looking all white and perfect.

I was like, "That ain't yours."

"It is so. We got a Yamaha snowmobile, too."

"Where your parents?"

"They're eating salad bars at the Wagon Wheel."

"Where you from?"

"Oconomowoc."

"Where's that?"

"Down by Milwaukee."

There was some snots running down his chin. I almost went over and wiped them but it was too skanky-looking.

I was like, "That coat's too big for you."

He said, "I'll grow into it."

"It's warm, ain't it."

He was like, "It's got antifreeze inside."

I went, "Antifreeze?"

"So you don't freeze."

I went, "You give it to me, maybe I'll start thinkin' about lettin' you go."

I went over and untied his hands. They was all trapped under his legs but I busted them knots loose pretty easy.

Up close he smelled like popcorn and grape gum.

Then he took off his puffy red coat and gave it to

me. Underneath his coat he was wearing a red sweater with snowflakes on it.

I was like, "You like that color, ain't it?"

He went, "Red's my favorite. I like blue, too."

Then Bruce sort of hugged himself for a minute and went, "I seen some policemen before, so you guys better be careful."

I was like, "Where?"

"In the game room. They were buying cigarettes from the machine."

I put his coat on and looked in the mirror. It fit me nice and tight. I could feel that antifreeze stuff heating up pretty crisp, too.

I was like, "Looks good, right?"

Bruce went, "It looks better on me."

When I peeked through the curtains there was a brown Impala in the parking lot. It had a Wisconsin State Police sign on the door. It was way off to the left where you would miss it if you didn't look hard enough. The color brown is like that. Maybe it's cuz that's the color of mud and dog shit.

When I turned back around little Bruce was picking his nose.

I was like, "Where's your pants, anyway?"

"Reggie took 'em off and then he put my shoes back on. He said we were gonna play a game."

I went, "What game?"

Bruce said, "The no-pants game. He took my shoes but he traded them back to me for the gobstopper. He was about to give me my pants for the Hot Tamales, too, but this girl came in the room and then they left with the puppy. She was real dirty-looking."

I looked down at his kicks. They was black Adidas soccer shoes.

I was like, "What size you wear?"

"Four in a half."

"You play soccer?"

"No, but I'm gonna."

I was like, "You're lucky they're too small; I'd take them joints, too."

Bruce kinda put one shoe one top of the other after I said that.

Then I went, "Them underwears is the wackest shit I ever seen."

"They were my Uncle Skyler's. He lives in Canada and he can hold his breath underwater longer than anyone."

I went, "They look like somethin' a nigger would wear."

Then he was like, "You're gonna go to hell."

I was like, "You don't know shit."

I looked out the window at that brown Impala. There was a pig in it this time. He was hanging his arm out the window and smoking a cigarette. I turned back to Bruce and he was wiggling his knees again.

I went, "You gotta diarrhea or somethin'?"

He was like, "No."

"Then why you so scared?"

"I'm not skeert."

"Yes you is. Faggit."

"I'm not a faggit."

"Faggit faggit faggit."

Then he told me I was going to hell again.

He was like, "You're going straight to hell. Do not pass go. Do not collect two hundred dollars."

I went, "If you so rich how come you wearin' someone else's underwears?"

Bruce was like, "I dunno," and wiped his chin again.

"Your parents is cheap."

"They give me quarters for Ninja Destroyer. I can get to the fourth level."

"I should go over to the Wagon Wheel and shoot 'em. Cheap bitches."

Then Bruce started crying. His knees was wiggling even faster now, like he was pissing in his little checkered underwears. I just stood by the mirror and watched him for a minute. He made these little honking noises like a duck or some shit.

I went, "Don't be such a pussy, Bruce."

He was like, "I'm not a pussy," and just kept crying.

Then I saw his pants all bunched in the corner by the real TV. They was these clean blue corduroys, and when you touched them it was like you was touching one of those chairs you sit in at the movies. I went over and grabbed them and untied his wrists and ankles and helped him put them on. To tell you the truth, for a second I thought about taking them corduroys, but I kept looking at how sad and small his legs was and how his underwears was bunched funny and how he kept covering his face with his hands. Then, for some reason, he put his arms around my legs and I could feel them shaking through my pants.

That shit was kind of wack, but it was making me sad so I kind of put my hand on his Milwaukee Brewers hat and pushed it down further over his ears. Then I told him to stop being a pussy again and to go and he kept wanting to give me that baseball card with the nigger on it, but I kept thinking how you can't really do nothing with no baseball card, so I was like, "No," and shit.

"Please," he said. "Please take it."

I was like, "Okay," and let him make me keep it. He didn't even ask for his phony-ass space gun.

I kept his puffy red coat, too, cuz it was getting cold out and that antifreeze was working even better than it was when I first put it on.

"Here, take this," I said, handing him that picture of the deer I took from the truck.

Bruce looked at it for a second and went, "You still want me to hypmotize you?"

I was like, "No."

"You still want me to get you some food. I got more gobstoppers. I got Slim Jims, too."

Even though that shit would have tasted pretty good I was like, "Just go."

Then he did this little shuffle step with his feet and squatted kind of low and popped back up.

I was like, "What was that?"

"Macaroni dance. It's better with music."

Then he turned and left.

When I closed the door behind him it was like he *disappeared* and shit. I stood there for a minute and looked at the wallpaper. Them fish seemed different every time you looked at them, I swear. They was all dressed up in suits and capes and shit. Some of them had dancing canes and some of them had fancy haircuts and some of them was playing sexophones.

After a minute I went over to the window and pulled back the curtain again, but Bruce was gone. He probably ran all the way to the Wagon Wheel. His parents probably didn't even notice he was gone cuz they was too busy stuffing their faces at the salad bar.

All I could see was them trucks and that big white Winnebago fun home.

The brown Impala was gone, though, and that was a good sign. The sun was getting weak and everything was starting to look like metal.

Later I ate some Utz cheese and crackers that Curl got from the vending machines and we watched the real TV. It was a Trinitron and it had a pretty crisp remote.

Boobie wanted to watch the Weather Channel cuz

he said we needed to stay ahead of the storm. I didn't hear nothing about no storm, but Boobie was convinced that there was one coming.

Then, a few minutes later, this lady with big white teeth kept talking about early snow and how it might be the biggest snowfall in northern Wisconsin history.

Boobie kept pulling the curtain back cuz I told him about that brown Impala with the Wisconsin State Police sign on the door and how the pig was smoking with his arm all hanging out the window and shit.

Boobie didn't look like he was doing too good, cuz his eyes was all big and scared and he kept staring at me. It was one of them stares that makes you feel like you got glass in your stomach. I just kept studying them fish and snapping and unsnapping my gat pocket. You could still hear Curl keeping the baby's hands away from her titties and you could hear the air conditioner and you could hear trucks parking and not-parking and you could hear that lady with the big white teeth talking on the TV.

My new puffy red coat was looking pretty crisp, though. I had to lie to Boobie about Bruce. I told him that while I was taking a shit I heard the door close and when I came back out Bruce was gone but his coat was there; that he probably had to wiggle out of it to get them shoelaces untied. Then I showed him that baseball card with the nigger on it and I showed him Bruce's talking space gun and Boobie just looked at that stuff and shook his head. Then he smoked a Basic and lit another and when he was finished with the second one he started pushing his fist in his eye.

Part of me wanted to go in the bathroom with Curl cuz the way he kept pushing his fist into his eye was making everything feel all small and fast like in a dream when you're getting chased but you keep falling.

I started doing a thirty-three in my head.

First I counted too quick and I was skipping numbers and shit, but I slowed down after I got to twelve.

For some reason I kept thinking about how things was good back in the tent and how the woods was like our crib and shit. But then I started hearing the road hissing by but it wasn't the road outside the otel Motel, it was the road that was going under the Skylark. And it wasn't just the road that already hissed, it was all the roads that was about to hiss when we'd start driving again. It was like that hiss was just part of everything now.

Then I started thinking about that newspaper article me and Curl seen when we was buying Boobie's Basics in North Caledonia and that hiss got bigger.

For a minute I thought it was gonna change into a migration headache, but it didn't. It just stayed a hiss and Boobie just kept sitting there pushing his fist into his eye.

When that antifreeze started getting too hot I took my puffy red coat off and hung it over a chair. I could feel Boobie's big dark eyes on me.

For some reason, I pulled the covers back and got

in the bed. The sheets was all cool and clean. You could smell the feathers in the pillows.

I asked Boobie if he was okay, but he just turned back to the window.

I thought about Bruce for a while; how he was in that Winnebago fun home and how he was probably sitting at the kitchen table, eating Count Chocula cereal or some shit. It was like he was still talking to me.

"You're going directly to hell," he was saying. "Do not pass go. Do not collect two hundred dollars."

I woke up behind the otel Motel. At first I didn't know where I was. All I could see was them big hairy trees and a Dumpster. There was so many stars they was making the sky look purple. The moon was like one of them Rockdale movie perverts breathing on you.

I was laying on a old torn-up mattress that was left next to the Dumpster. I was wearing my Pro Flyers and Bruce's puffy red coat, but other than that I was naked.

The last thing I remembered was how Curl pulled the baby out of the TV cuz he wouldn't stop crying and how crowded we all was in the bed and how them feathers in the pillows was smelling all clean and powdery.

As soon as I stood up I knew I had a migration headache. It was like I got stabbed in the brain. I walked around to the front. I had to use my hand to push off the side of the Dumpster for balance. When I saw the pink otel Motel sign blinking it hurt my eyes so bad I almost fell against the Coke machine.

There wasn't nobody back in the room and all of the sudden everything started to feel like it was going too fast. I found my pants under the chair and pulled them over my Pro Flyers. My gat was still in the leg pocket so that was a good sign.

At first I thought Boobie and Curl skated cuz the room felt all big and empty and them wallpaper fish looked all evil like they was laughing at me, so I started crying like a little bitch, like Winnebago Bruce from Oconomowoc. But after a minute I saw the keys to the Skylark on top of the baby's TV and I cooled out.

I sat on the end of the bed for a minute. My migration headache was pounding. All you could hear was some cars hissing down the highway. It was like they was hissing right through my brain meat.

I went into the bathroom and grabbed a toothpaste cup and skated. I had to be careful cuz at the other end of the otel Motel there was all this broken glass on the sidewalk.

I walked up to each door and put my toothpaste cup against it like they do in the movies. All you could hear was people snoring and shifting around in their beds.

In room 6B there was some light coming through a crack in the curtain and you could hear voices. I put my toothpaste cup right up against the window.

Even though I had that migration headache I could hear pretty good.

First you could hear Curl, and then you could hear this man whose voice sounded like some furniture getting dragged across the floor. I couldn't tell if Curl was laughing or crying.

I started to feel like if I kept listening I would get stuck there, so I left.

Back in our room I locked myself in the bathroom. The bathroom's the only place you can go if you ever want to feel okay, cuz toilets make you feel safe cuz of how cool the water feels when you float your hand in them.

I used to do that at the Rockdale post office when I'd get scared. I'd just creep into a stall and float my hand and it always made me feel better.

But back in Little Chicago, even though I was floating my hand in the toilet, my face kept getting hotter and everything kept going all sweaty and spinning, and then my stomach started screaming, but I couldn't eat them screams cuz that migration headache was messing with my insides. The next thing I knew I was spitting up yellow. It looked like this Mr. Clean stuff I used to use to mop Old Man Turpentine's Fun Shop floor and it tasted like paint and it burped out of me for about five minutes.

After that yellow junk stopped coming out of me I just sat down on the floor and did some thirty-threes.

Curl's voice was in the room now, going, "Quit! Quit, you!"

You could hear the baby squeaking, too. Them voices mixing with my thirty-threes started to make everything slow down.

Then the door closed and Curl got all quiet.

You could hear Boobie now, too. He asked Curl where she was. His voice was all deep and quiet so you could barely hear it. Curl just said how she wasn't *nowhere* and then everything went dead for a minute and my mind got stuck trying to figure out how the baby got back in the room. Boobie must have been trying to sell him in the parking lot while Curl was working that man in room 6B.

Then Curl told Boobie how she got some money and you could hear him smack her.

Curl started going, "No, Boobie, no!" and "I got twenty thick, Boobie. Twenty thick!" and then there was them sounds that fists make when they bust a face and some furniture moving and something up against the door and then something falling off the dresser and crashing and Curl eating her crying and then everything went dead again.

When I came out, Curl was standing next to the Trinitron and she was leaning funny and she was chewing gum all slow and ugly. She was wearing my Pro Flyer that fell off and holding her face and she was only like six inches away from the wall. She was chewing that gum so hard it was like it was the only thing keeping her from leaving. Her sunflower dress was all crooked and you could see the twenty dollars from her trick scattered on the floor.

For some reason Curl kept reaching up and touching the wallpaper. It was like the only thing that she knew was them fish. And she was all quiet and lopsided like she gets after she does some bazooka. Curl's eyes was so big it was like she got turned into a *doll*.

I walked over to her and put my hand on her arm.

She went, "Hey, Custis," and kept chewing her gum.

I was like, "Hey," and just stood there.

The curtains was twisted and the mattress was half off the bed and the Bible was spread in the middle of the floor like a smashed bird. Curl just kept staring at the wallpaper.

The baby was crying but I couldn't see him.

Curl reached over and grabbed my hand.

She went, "You sleep okay?"

I just nodded and kept looking for the baby's TV.

Then she went, "You hungry?" and her voice sounded like it was trapped in a French fry bag.

I was like, "I'm okay."

Then Curl went, "You goin' back to bed?" but I didn't answer and you could tell she didn't really care cuz she was too busy staring at the wallpaper.

Some car lights shined in the room and lit up them wallpaper fish. Somehow them wallpaper fish looked scared, too.

Then I saw the baby's TV. It was turned over on the other side of the bed and it was cracked and the baby wasn't in it but you could still hear it crying.

Then Curl talked again. She went, "Tomorrow we're gonna go swimming in the pool, ain't we, Boobie?" but Boobie wasn't even there.

Curl went, "They got a swimming pool out back. And the water's bluer than blue."

She said the water was so blue she seen a *quarter* in it, and then she gave me my Pro Flyer. Her foot just sort of kicked it toward me like it had its own brain and shit.

Some more car lights shined into the room and that's when I saw the baby. He was underneath the bed in his shitted diaper, and his arms and legs was all swimming out like one of them Des Plaines River turtles that gets flipped on its back.

Then Boobie came back in the room with a big book of matches. I looked at him and then down at the baby. Boobie's face was so still it looked painted.

I went, "Hey, Boobie."

He didn't say nothing back so I was like, "Hey, Boobie, you okay?" but he just kept staring.

Then for some reason I went, "You got any gum?"

I don't know why I said that shit. I think it's cuz I could smell how sweet Curl's breath was.

Then Boobie came over to us and opened Curl's mouth and took her gum and he put it in *my* mouth and held his hand over my face and made me chew. It tasted like spit and it tasted purple and it tasted kind of like a pencil, too.

Then Boobie went into the bathroom and started lighting matches.

That's when I reached under the bed and got the baby. He grabbed onto my thumb and wouldn't let go. The seam in his forehead was dirty so I cleaned it with some spit, and then I bounced him in my arms and sang that "Hushabye Mountain" song till he stopped crying.

You could smell the matches burning in the bathroom pretty thick.

I was like, "Curl, you smell that?" but she didn't answer. She was too busy staring at the wallpaper.

When Boobie came out of the bathroom that book of matches was burning right in his hand. He walked a few steps and then he dropped it in the middle of the bed and it caught fire and he just stood there and watched it for a minute. Curl kept watching the wallpaper fish and I was frozen with the baby. After a minute the feathers in the pillows was on fire, too, and they was flying all over the room like electric snow.

When the fire started crawling off the bed and onto the floor, the alarm went off. Boobie grabbed the baby's TV and pulled Curl toward the door.

Everything was all wack for a second, but I had the baby and I had my red puffy coat and I had both of my Pro Flyers.

It only took us like twenty seconds to get back in the Skylark.

I was glad I had that puffy red coat, cuz it was getting seriously cold out.

When we pulled away from the parking lot I looked back at our room. You could see how that electric snow was falling across the window. You could see the little otel Motel sign blinking pink and you could see how them flames in room 4 was already licking up the curtains.

CURL

My Aunty Frisco used to say
that a man who hits a dog
is likely to kick it in a month.

Boobie

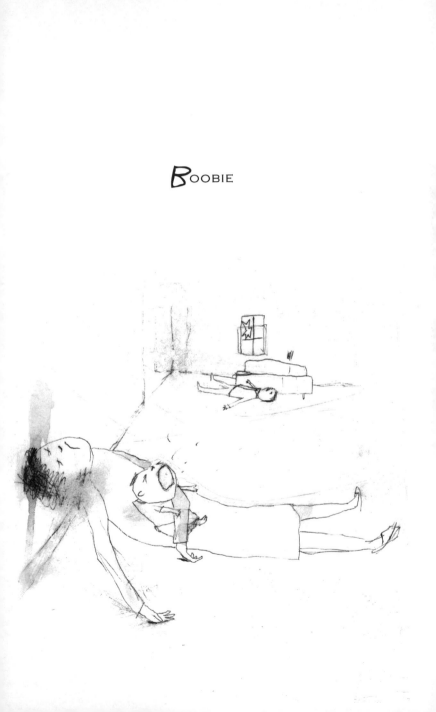

THE VAN

CUSTIS

The snow's coming down sideways. Curl says *horizontal* but I just say sideways cuz it's easier to say. I think horizontal is the biggest word she knows. And she says it all slow, too, just to make it sound fancy.

We've been living in the van for a week. It ain't nothing like the tent. It ain't even like the Skylark. It's just a old, torn-up school van that don't got no tires. It's so old it ain't even yellow no more. It's just this wack non-color.

Most of the windows is smashed and all of the back seats is missing. The inside smells like one of them dead refrigerators from Renfro Park. The whole van leans to the left kind of lopsided like it's trying to listen to them other cars hissing on the highway.

We sleep at the back end, where the van don't lean too bad. We found some couch cushions behind this furniture store off of Highway 227. When you line them cushions up right it ain't so bad. But when they spread apart that crooked metal floor feels like a brick in the middle of your back.

For a table we flipped a paint can and stuck a stop sign on top. It gets bumped every time Boobie skates for his Basics, but it makes you feel like it's a official crib. It's like there ain't no real life inside a place if you don't got no table.

Curl had to stop changing the baby's diaper cuz her hands ain't been working right. Somewhere back in Wisconsin she caught a lung frost. And it's gotten worse in the last few days. Right after we skated from the otel Motel that coughing started.

According to the map we're in this place called Nimrod, Minnesota, by the Detroit Lakes. Curl tried telling me that Detroit is in Michigan but she can't read the map cuz her eyes is so bad. I'm the one who does all the reading now.

Before we got to Nimrod we drove by the Frames Landing Campground. I tried to get Boobie to let us stay there cuz there was other people with families and we'd be able to make friends and steal shit, but he just kept shaking his head and talking about how where we needed to be was as close to nowhere as possible.

And Nimrod's about as close to nowhere as I've ever seen. There ain't nothing here but snow and trees and these birds that is so tough they don't even gotta fly south and shit.

Once in a while you hear a car going by way off on Highway 71 but that's about it. I seen some jets one day, too. They was silver and there was three of them and when they flew by it was so loud it almost busted the drums in my ears.

The cold ain't helping Curl's lung frost none. When she sleeps you can see that froggy heartbeat going slower and slower in her eye. And sometimes you just sit there and count it cuz you think counting it'll keep it from going too slow. Sometimes it goes so slow you think you can *hear* it and shit.

Everything she tries to eat just gets spit back up all over her sunflower dress. There ain't no doubt that that bazooka's got her stomach now. Her ribs is so big they look like claws trying to bust through her sides. I try talking about food, like Ding Dongs and Nutty Bars and Little Tonio microwave burritos, just to see if it might make her ribs go back down, but she just looks away and stares off with them big froggy eyes.

I even told her about this skinny little snowfish I seen swimming in the Crow Wing River, way over by where Boobie hides the Skylark. I told her how it was doing somersaults and flipping its fins around. And I told her how I was going to catch it and give it to her so she could gut it and clean it and cook it up, but she just half-smiled so you could see how her teeth is turning gray.

It don't help that it started snowing sideways.

Every time Curl coughs it sounds like her lung bubbles is tearing. Boobie keeps her wrapped in this sheepskin coat he stole from a Wendy's when we was still back in Wisconsin. We was just about to cross the border on Highway 2 and big-ass Lake Superior was all huge and icy-looking off in the distance when he saw that rest-stop sign and pulled over. He walked into the Wendy's in his plain white T-shirt and walked out with that sheepskin coat and a big bag of French fries.

Now Boobie wears this old softball jacket that he found in the trunk of the Skylark. It's blue and it says "Elliot" on the chest.

The baby wears this little puffy snowsuit that Curl stole from this big outlet store off the highway. It's pink and it's got a hood. Sometimes we put this McDonald's napkin over his face so it don't get frostbit. We make sure to poke a hole in it so he can breathe. It's weird cuz it makes the baby look like a doll that never got finished. Sometimes I have to look under it cuz I get this spooky-ass feeling that his face has disappeared. It's always there, though.

We've been keeping a coffee can lit in the back of the van and that fire gets to blazing pretty crisp sometimes, but Curl just keeps shaking and coughing. And she picks at her hands so hard it's like she's trying to pull the moons out of her fingernails. The only time she leaves the van is to shit and piss.

Boobie taped newspapers to the windows to keep the snow out. We found some old yellow curtains that was in the trunk of the Skylark, too, but we only put one of them on the window. Curl uses the other one as a blanket.

We all sleep in our clothes. My pants feel like they've growed right over my skin. And I got a bruise on my leg from my gat.

Even though she knows she ain't supposed to get no colder, every night Curl wakes me up and begs me to pull one of them newspapers back cuz she thinks there's a big black turkey hopping around outside the van. She says it's got monster wings and that she can hear it dancing on the roof. She says she can feel how that black turkey wants to reach inside her chest with one of its long greasy turkey toes and steal her heart.

But every time I pull the newspapers back there ain't nothing there. Curl says it flies away when I look cuz it can read my thoughts or some shit. I know all that black turkey stuff ain't nothing but maybe some dream Curl had, but I still play along with the newspaper game almost every night just to make her feel better.

After the first sideways snow all the birds that ain't tough flew away in big boomerangs. Then the trees died. Curl says the trees died cuz birds got medicine in their wings that keeps the trees alive. Sometimes at night you can hear them dead trees breathing.

Yesterday Boobie scraped some cough syrup from a Amoco station in this town called Oylen, but all that did was make Curl fall asleep twice as long. And she slept so hard we was afraid she wasn't gonna wake up. She was so still shit got kind of scary for a minute. That froggy heartbeat in her eye almost stopped like four times. Boobie had to draw on her with a marker to make her wake up. For some reason he drew a fish. He drew it right on her face, too. That shit looked kinda spooky and dead to me. Maybe it's cuz he gave the fish a X instead of a eye. For some reason it made Curl wake up.

When Boobie wasn't looking I tried to wipe that fish off of Curl's face with some snow, but I couldn't get it all the way, so every time you look at her now, the first thing you see is that froggy heartbeat and the second thing you see is that picture of the fish with the X for a eye.

Curl told me that if I find a bird I should kill it and take all the feathers off and put them over her heart. She says there's medicine in bird feathers and that it's the only way to make her lung frost go away.

When I went bird hunting yesterday I saw this little farm that had this wack-looking chicken hopping in the dirt. It looked more like a rat with feathers than a chicken.

That farm was in the middle of *nowhere* and shit. The only thing around it was this big old black forest that looked like all the trees was burnt. It didn't look like nobody lived there but a ghost or maybe one of them Big Foot freaks you see in comic book pictures and shit.

Tomorrow I'm going to roll by there and steal that chicken for Curl. I know a chicken ain't no real bird cuz of how chickens don't fly, but it's close enough, and it don't seem like Curl's got time to be choosy, cuz along with them yellow smears under her eyes her piss is turning brown.

Back in Rockdale this old skanky sucker who hung out by the water tower called Joe Greenway got brown piss and he died like four days later.

Last night Boobie stayed up with Curl all night trying to get her to eat some soup, but she just kept spitting it up. That lung frost poison ain't letting nothing stay in her body. The baby sure liked the soup, though.

When you look through the windows some of the dead trees look like giant monster claws scratching at the sky. Others look like old, crooked dinosaur bones that got cooked by a fire.

Curl says that if you walk too close to them trees they'll kidnap you. She says that even though they don't got no eyes you can feel them looking.

She says one night she woke up and saw them dead trees running around. She says they only run around like that when they think you're sleeping.

It's like that big black turkey and them running trees is the only shit Curl cares about now.

She said she saw a movie once where a tree ran down a hill and killed this man cuz he tried to chop it down with a axe. She said it ran right down that hill like it had some kicks on.

At night the sky glows purple like the light from a TV when a VCR movie is done playing. And the stars get so big they look like knives coming at you. Some of them stars look like spaceships, too. Especially them blue ones.

It would be cool if one of them blue stars came and a spaceman lit up his insides and showed us his moon bones. We'd let him stay with us for a few days. We'd give him some of Boobie's Basics and let him mess with the baby so he could study him and learn about Earth. Curl says the best way to learn about humans is by studying babies cuz they ain't been fucked or starved yet.

Them spacemen probably got some pretty cool stuff on their spaceship, too—like them video games you play with helmets and rocks that tell the future and computers and robots that can sing Pepsi-Cola commercials and shit.

And if things go pretty smooth that spaceman might even invite us to go back with him, and he'd give us astronaut suits and put the baby in a little gravity crib with galaxy blankets and we'd leave the TV behind and skate with the aliens and the fire from the launch pad would make a big launch burn on the van and then—

blow! — our spaceship would blast off and like four seconds later the pigs would pull up in their Impalas and their Caprice Classics, like skeighty-eight of them suckers, and they'd jump out and slam the doors and watch our spaceship disappear through the purple sky like a little golden chicken egg.

That would be pretty crisp.

All Earth's got is a bunch of Joliet suckers and Rockdale suckers and pit bulls and shit, anyways. And the Joliet suckers poison the Rockdale suckers cuz they don't want them stealing their money, and when the Rockdale suckers die the pit bulls eat their bones, and then the Joliet suckers catch the pit bulls and turn them into hamburgers and French fries and eat them and they get so fat their money suits don't fit them no more, and then they gotta buy some new ones, and that's what it's all about down here on Earth — some rich Joliet suckers getting richer so they can buy cell phones and emails and fatter money suits.

Them spacemen probably got stronger hearts than humans, too, cuz they don't got no pit bull worries or no money suit worries or no Bob Motley worries. All them worries make your heart small, and the smaller your heart, the less it glows.

I think that's how come Jesus always has that glow around his hair in them Bible pictures — cuz his heart was so big it made his *head* light up and shit.

This one Rockdale hippie man called Jerry who hangs out down by the Speedway used to go around saying Jesus was a nigger and that all them people in the Bible was niggers. I told him how Bob Motley says you can't get no halo if you're a nigger cuz of all that motor oil they put in their hair, but Jerry just looked the other way and kept handing out Jesus pamphlets to all the suckers at the Speedway.

Bob Motley said that niggers don't got no hearts. He said that their chests is filled with donkey shit instead.

Curl says that you get a halo by growing your heart big, and that halos don't got nothing to do with the color of your skin.

When I'm in the van keeping Curl warm I get to thinking about everything that's happened; about all the driving and Dumpster diving and all them vending machines we tilted and that highway hiss and Boobie always putting green Gatorade down his dickhole cuz of his clap and the otel Motel and Curl's lung frost and the baby and about skeighty-eight other things and I get worried that one of them migration headaches is gonna come and never leave my head.

Doing them thirty-threes helps sometimes. Not all the time, but sometimes they do.

If it ain't too windy, once in a while you can hear a train whistle. And you're like, "Damn, a train," and you look around but all you see is trees.

Sometimes I wonder what happened to the little kids who was in the van. They probably got their heads chopped off or some shit.

I think some big tall man in a black coat walks over the earth with a axe, and when he finds some little kids crashed in a school van, he pulls them out all nice and friendly and they think he's going to use that axe to chop down a wall and save some little girl who's trapped, but then he lines them up shortest-to-tallest and talks to them all soft with that trust in his voice and maybe even gives them some gum or candy or a Susan B. Anthony silver dollar like Sidekick, and just when they think he's going to help them get back to their school he creeps up behind them and — *whop-whop-whop* — he chops their heads off instead.

Curl's lung frost smell is skanking up the van pretty bad. Boobie still does her, though — even with that yellow crawling under her eyes and her insides dripping all over her dress. It's cuz that love he's got for her is stronger than her lung frost. He won't french her, though, no matter how much Curl begs for it.

I saw her frenching her hand last night like she wished it was Boobie.

I guess that's cool.

When everything's all skanked and the trees is dead and you got a lung frost and the snow keeps falling sideways and you don't got nothing but a sheepskin and a couple of curtains to keep you warm, you can always french your hand.

CURL

A gentle breeze from Hushabye Mountain
Softly blows o'er Lullaby Bay
It fills the sails of boats that are waiting
Waiting to sail your worries away

It isn't far to Hushabye Mountain
And your boat waits down by the key
The winds of night so softly are sighing
Soon they will fly your troubles to sea

So close your eyes on Hushabye Mountain
Wave goodbye to cares of the day
Watch your boat from Hushabye Mountain
Sail far away from Lullaby Bay

BOOBIE

CUSTIS

That old nigger man just sneaked up on me with his rusty rifle going, "Go 'head and touch it. Go on." And his voice was all oily and wack like a voice you hear when you're hiding on the Metra Rock Island train to Chicago and the conductor is coming to bust your ass.

My hand is shaking and that old nigger's eyes is so white it's like God made them like that on purpose just to scare little kids. And now I got my gat pulled out and I realize that my snap must've got stuck again cuz the whole pocket's ripped and the snap's jammed in the trigger and now I got my gat pointed at that chicken and that ratty little bird ain't jumping around like them chickens you see on TV — this one's staring at me the way a poker player stares at you when he's got a flush and its eye is all hard and dark like a doll's eye so I squeeze the trigger three times but my gat won't fire probably cuz of the snow going sideways and shit and after the old nigger with the rifle sees how wack my gat is he starts moving toward me all slow and evil and he's bow-legged and skinny and creaky-looking like one of them homeless bummy Rockdale niggers and that makes his moving toward me seem twice as slow and twice as evil so I try shooting the chicken again but my gat just makes that little noise like some bird bones snapping and then the nigger tells me if I do the trigger one more time he's gonna pull my pants down and paddle my ass so hard with the end of his rifle that I ain't gonna be able to walk for the rest of my life and his voice is all deep and tired and kinda spooky like he's been hiding in a basement for like skeighty-eight years and shit so I put my gat back in my leg pocket and he tells me the only thing he hates worse than a thief is a chicken thief and how his wack little chicken is older than me and how he named it after his wife and how he's gonna tie a rope around my ankle and make me clean his yard and how he ain't gonna untie the rope till the whole thing is cleaned and how the chicken is gonna watch me and peck on the window if I start messing with the rope and then I look at his yard and there's all this wack shit in it like tin cans and grocery bags and it's all wet and slimy from the snow. And now that old nigger's holding that ankle rope he was talking about like he thought about it with his mind and it just appeared out of that thought and he's tying that rope all tight around my ankle and he's the tallest nigger I've ever seen like at least seven feet and his hand with the rope is bigger than a clock and that chicken keeps staring at me and then the nigger takes my wrist in his big nasty hand and he touches some blood from where my gat scraped me and he pulls out a snot rag and wraps it around my wrist and makes a knot so it stops bleeding and then he turns around and grabs this big skanky plastic bag and hands it to me and I take it and it smells like something dead was living in it and then he turns around again all slow and creaky like he might fall and he walks back to his little house with the other end of the rope and the light from the window turns all yellow and warm like the light you see in a spoon when there's some honey on it and the sideways snow starts to come down thicker and through the window I can see that old nigger just rocking back and forth in front of a fireplace and you can see some flames sawing and he's got the rope tied to the rocking chair now and he's rubbing his legs like they hurt and the chicken just keeps staring at me with that doll's eye and then things start to slow down for some reason.

I think it's cuz of how you can smell the smoke falling all warm and sweet from the nigger's chimney and how that yellow honey light is glowing on the window.

So I back away from the chicken real slow, one, two, three.

That doll's eye is staring so hard you can feel it like a bug on your arm.

Then I do a thirty-three and start to clean the nigger's yard.

When I finish cleaning the yard he comes walking out of his house carrying a brown paper bag.

The snow is still coming down sideways and it looks all wack bouncing off his black-ass head. My hands is cold and my toes is numb and I can't feel my nose too good and my pants is all wet from slipping in the wetness. I can't even feel that rope around my ankle no more. I got that big skanky garbage bag half-full of snow and half-full of all that shit from his yard.

He just stands there with that brown paper bag and stares at me for a second. He's so tall he's like one of them burnt trees from that forest.

He goes, "You like sneakin' around in folks's chicken hutches?"

I go, "No," and clear some snow out of my eyes.

The old nigger looks at his big hand for some reason and goes, "Shoo. You must."

I don't say nothing. I just stare at his old oily head.

Then he goes, "How old are you?"

I'm like, "Old enough."

"Nine? Ten?"

"Twenty-seven."

Then he kind of smiles and goes, "You ain't even twelve."

I just stand there and go, "You don't know shit."

And he's like, "I don't, huh?"

"You're just a creaky old nigger."

"Am I really?"

"Yep."

"Your momma teach you that word?"

"Nope."

"My lord. A ten-year-old chicken thief with a ugly heart. Ain't never seen that before."

For some reason I go, "Wack."

And he's all like, "Goodness gracious," like he can't cuss cuz we're in *church* or some shit.

I just stand there feeling that rope cutting into my ankle. The old nigger stands there too and wipes some motor oil off his head with a rag.

Then he goes, "What do you want with my chicken?"

I'm like, "Nothin."

"You was gonna eat it?"

"No."

"Sell it?"

"Nope."

"You was gonna swap it at the hock shop? They only got one hock shop around here. It's about thirty miles away."

I don't even know what a hock shop is, so I just go, "I was gonna give it to my friend."

"Your friend a chicken collector?"

"She's sick."

"What she want with a chicken?"

"She said there's stuff in its wings."

"Stuff?"

"Yep."

"What stuff?"

"Medicine?"

"She a witch?"

"No."

Then he tries to crack a joke and shit. He goes, "She got a broomstick?"

But I don't even flinch. I just go, "She said birds got medicine in their wings."

He goes, "Deuce ain't gonna do nothin' but bite her in her fanny."

Then we don't say nothing again. We just stand there and watch each other. I look over at his window and I can see that fire in the fireplace and that yellow light and the end of that rope still tied to his rocking chair.

Then the old nigger bends kind of low and looks at that snot rag he tied around my wrist. He pats it a few times with his long, bony fingers. Then he points to my leg pocket.

He goes, "You got good luck in that pocket?"

I'm like, "I ain't got nothin' in my pocket."

And he's like, "Nothin' but a half-broke cap gun."

"If it worked I'd shoot your old creaky ass."

"Lord, I'm sure you would."

"I would."

"You hateful."

"You're lucky it's snowing."

Then the nigger shakes his head like Sister Blister used to after I'd do something to one of them retards. He shakes it about four times and goes, "Goodness gracious, goodness gracious."

Then he points to my other pocket and goes, "What's wrong with your hand?"

I go, "I cut it."

But he's like, "I mean the one in your pocket."

I go, "Nothin'."

"You steal somethin' from my yard?"

"Ain't shit to steal."

"You sure?"

I'm like, "You deaf?"

And then the nigger pulls my other hand out of my pocket and he looks at it.

He goes, "You know you got frostbite?"

I just pull it back and go, "That's cuz I stuck it in your mama's pussy."

Then the nigger laughs this big scratchy laugh and goes, "Goodness gracious, goodness gracious," a few more times and then we are silent.

After a minute he goes, "What's your name?"

I'm like, "Why?"

He goes, "Never knew nobody called Why before."

Then he laughs again and hands me the brown paper bag and goes, "You poke garbage pretty fair, Mr. Why."

I'm like, "I ain't no garbage poker."

"My yard ain't been this clean since I can't remember." He looks at me for a second. "Where you from, anyway?"

"Nowhere."

"Nowhere, huh?"

"Yep."

"You just up and come out of Nowhere."

"I guess."

Then he looks at me kind of sideways and goes, "They must make pretty good-looking winter coats in Nowhere."

I go, "They must."

"I don't know how you managed to get frostbite with a coat like that."

I don't say nothing after that. For some reason, I open that brown bag instead and there's a piece of apple pie in it.

The nigger's like, "Apple brown Betty ain't about bein' petty," but I don't know what that means neither, so I just take a big bite out of it and it tastes so good it's like there's a radio going in my mouth. There's cinnamon and raisins and apples and all types of flavors in it.

He goes, "Don't eat it too fast or you'll get jumpy."

I take another bite and I put the piece of pie back in the brown bag.

Then the nigger wipes some more motor oil off his

face and I look back at the window. I can see them flames sawing all slow and orange in the fireplace.

Then he starts holding his side like it hurts and goes, "I could use a extra hand around here. The way my legs give out anymore. You need a job?"

I go, "I don't need shit from you, Blacky."

He just shakes his head and says, "Little Jimster with a mean shoulder."

"My name ain't Jimster."

Then he bends real low and starts rubbing his shins and his face changes like it hurts.

Then he goes, "You could come by and help me a bit," still rubbing his shins.

I don't say nothing back. I just look at the snow and how it's piling up so high it looks like the sky's dropping.

Then the old nigger scratches his head again and goes, "I'd give you some food. Put a meal in your belly. Toast with jam. Biscuits with sausage."

But I just stand there.

Then he finishes rubbing his shins and stands up straight and jangles some change in his pocket and it sounds like music snow would make if snow could make music, and then he goes, "I might even give you some quarters."

But I still don't say nothing back.

Then the nigger smiles that big smile again and his teeth light up all white and perfect and he asks me my name again and I go, "Why?" and he just shakes his head and says, "Thanks for cleaning my yard, Mr. Why. Mr. Why from Nowhere."

Then he takes the rope off my ankle and tells me to come on by tomorrow and that he's got a bunch of pennies in jars that he needs to roll, but I don't say nothing cuz that rope made a red mark around my ankle and it's still snowing sideways and the snowflakes is bouncing off the old nigger's head like little white BB's, and when I start to back away he's still smiling that big shiny-ass smile, going, "Goodness gracious, goodness gracious."

When I got back the whole van smelled like paint. Boobie was changing the baby and the baby was squeaking and swimming out and Boobie's big hands was busy folding up a diaper and taping them sticker strips down. And his hands looked twice as big, cuz I ain't never seen them moving over the baby like that.

You could see Boobie's breath going and the baby's breath going underneath.

The van was snowing. It wasn't snowing sideways yet, but it was definitely snowing. Them flakes was floating down just like we was outside.

Curl was in the back under the curtains. She was shaking all fast and electric and clawing at her fingers and her eyes was froggier than ever and it looked like she wasn't getting no air.

Her breath was leaking out of her mouth the way

smoke leaks out of a ashtray and it was leaking so slow you could see it bending to the left. The light in her eyes looked like it was fading, too. She just kept shaking and trying to not-shake and you could hear that lung frost killing her.

Boobie pulled back the newspapers cuz the paint smell was so strong. That's how them flakes was drifting into the van. But with Curl's lung frost going double and the baby's TV getting colder, the snow floating in the van didn't seem right.

The can of black spray paint we used on the Skylark was rolling around on the floor and the top was off.

At first I thought Curl was breathing them paint fumes to get lifted. But then I looked on the walls and there was all these little spray paint drawings. I couldn't tell what them drawings was cuz they was mostly squiggles.

I went to the back of the van and sat down next to Curl and gave her that brown paper bag with the old nigger's pie in it. That fish was still on her face looking spookier than ever. She just stared at the piece of apple pie with them big froggy eyes and shook her head. You could tell she wanted to eat it just by the way her eyes got big. But it was like something inside wouldn't let her. Something that didn't have nothing to do with bazooka or lung frosts or getting lifted. It was like *God* wouldn't let her eat that pie — like he took her stomach away and stuck a dead snake in it instead.

After a minute her big froggy eyes just closed and

she swallowed this little swallow and you could see the muscles jumping in her throat.

She kept falling asleep and trying to not-sleep and that froggy heartbeat in her eye kept going slower and slower.

I just sat real close to her and watched how the van was snowing.

Once Curl opened her eyes and we both smiled cuz it was like we got psychic for a second, and even though that thought we shared was kinda sad and kinda scary and had something to do with how that froggy heartbeat in her eye kept going slower and slower and how that lung frost poison was sinking deeper in her, it was still cool cuz we shared it.

The next time Curl opened her eyes I offered her the pie again, but she just waved it off like before.

Then I told her about the old nigger's little rickety farm and how I tried to steal the chicken and how I had to clean his yard and how I kept slipping and how I got snow all up in my crack and shit and she laughed at me and her laughs sounded kind of like crying and then she was eating her laugh-cries and then she was coughing out them laugh-cries that she ate but her coughs was so weak they was more like whispers than coughs. I felt like crying, too, but I ain't no little bitch so I didn't.

I told Curl how that chicken had that doll's eye and I showed her the red mark that the old nigger's rope left on my leg, and she put her hand on it and she even

113

rubbed her thumb over the redness for a second and it seemed like she wanted to talk but she couldn't. I bent my head real close to her mouth so I could hear what she was trying to say, but all she said was, "Little brother, little brother" real quiet and small.

Then her eyes closed for a while and when they opened again I asked her what all them squiggles on the walls was and she made these little falling movements with her fingers the way snow falls so I went, "Snow?" and she nodded and then she made these other movements with her hands and them movements was like birds maybe so I was like, "Birds?" but she shook her head and did them hand movements again and it was like fish swimming so I went, "Fish?" and she nodded again and smiled, and even though her teeth was kind of dim and skanky it was the prettiest smile Curl ever made.

Then Curl grabbed my hand with the frostbite and started humming and Boobie held the baby and started even rocking it a little and the van was snowing worst and the Moon was all lopsided and strange in the window like a big skanky shark heart.

After Curl died, me and Boobie sat in the van and ate our crying. His didn't make no sound, but mine was all wack like a dog getting kicked.

When her heart stopped you could hear it the way you can hear the rides shut down when the Joliet Knights of Columbus Summer Carnival ends. The sunflower on her dress looked like it grew; like it used the little bit of life she had left as food to get bigger.

Her arms was reached over her head and her legs was all stretched and spread out like she was trying to make a snow angel.

We taped the newspapers back to the window but the van was still snowing. It was coming through the cracks now, and where there weren't no cracks it was just coming anyways.

My frostbite hand was aching like crazy. Sometimes it burnt and sometimes it ached. I could see how the side of it was turning kinda black.

Boobie put the TV between us on the floor and I let the baby chew on my thumb. He didn't cry the whole time. It's funny how babies only cry when they're hungry or they gotta shit. A plane could crash or someone could die and it don't mean nothing to them. They just stare off with them little blue eyes, wondering when them bananas and milk is coming.

I stared at them squiggles Curl spray-painted for a long time and it made me sleepy. You could see the frost moving over them like a shadow creeping.

Boobie ate his crying all night. You could barely hear it. He ate his crying till there wasn't no more to eat.

I fell asleep doing a thirty-three.

When we woke up the wind was sneaking through the cracks and the van was snowing worst. It got so cold that that frost climbing over the walls started turning white.

We put the baby in the TV and headed for the Skylark. That walk felt like one of the longest walks of my life. The snow was slippery and I fell down on my frostbite hand about skeighty-eight times.

My ears was full of snow and my eyes was full of snow and my Pro Flyers was so wet it was like I was walking in a river.

Once we reached the Skylark everything was cool cuz Boobie started the engine and the windshield wipers were going and after a few minutes the heat kicked in and we was warm.

Through the windshield that snow just kept coming. You couldn't see *shit*. Not no trees. Not no Crow Wing River. Just all that snow blowing sideways. It was like that shit was *sliding*. Like it was avalanching from off the top of a *mountain*.

After a while you could tell that being warm wasn't going to change nothing. It was like there was a new kind of coldness inside you. It wasn't no coldness that had to do with the weather. It was the kind of coldness that lives under the world, in a big black cave, with a bunch of bats and lost bones and shit.

We couldn't just start driving again with Curl back there in the van. We couldn't just get lost in that highway hiss again. Driving just didn't seem right without Curl.

For a minute, the snow stopped falling sideways. You could barely see the Crow Wing River and how it was all frozen over like a little mirror. Boobie stared at it for a long time and his eyes was all big and sad and scared-looking.

I asked him what we was gonna do with Curl, but he didn't have no answer, so I just let the baby chew on my thumb and waited for him to do something.

But Boobie's black eyes just kept turning blacker.

After a while the snow started sliding sideways again. It wasn't like this snow was just coming from the clouds and the sky. It was like the snow was coming from the trees and the ground and the Crow Wing River, too. It was like the snow was coming from *everywhere* and *nowhere* all at the same time.

Then Boobie undid my pocket and pulled out my gat, and he looked at it for a minute all small and wack in his hand and the wipers was moving faster on the windshield and I was all quiet and scared cuz I didn't know what Boobie was gonna do, and the baby started crying cuz he shitted his diaper again and you could smell it and that seam in his forehead looked like a little muscle muscling between his eyes, and then Boobie took my good hand and put it over his hand and put my gat up to his chest with my hand over his hand which was over my gat and it was happening so fast it was like it wasn't even happening and I could feel his heart pounding through his chest *thuddump* and through my gat *thuddump* and through his hand *thuddump* and through my hand *thuddump* and it was beating so strong it was like you could taste it beating in your mouth so I closed my eyes and then Boobie squeezed the trigger but nothing happened cuz of the snow and then he tried it again and I felt like I was falling and there wasn't no sound but the windshield wipers.

When I opened my eyes Boobie wasn't in the driver's seat no more. He wasn't next to me and he wasn't in the back seat neither, and then I looked up and through the windshield I could see him walking backwards through the dead trees.

I looked in the back seat again cuz I couldn't hear the baby but the TV was still there and the baby was in it and his arms was swimming out and you could see the windshield wipers slashing through his little blue eyes and I gave him my frostbite hand and he took it and put it in his mouth and I tried singing that "Hushabye Mountain" song to him but I couldn't get the words right cuz my teeth was chattering.

Then I looked out through the windshield again and Boobie kept walking backwards, smaller and smaller, and the snow was thick and white and sideways but you could still see how his hair was lifting off his shoulders. He raised his hand up like he was trying to say good-bye and even though he was far away now I put my good hand up and tried to touch him through the glass.

And I called out to him, too. I used the voice in my throat and the voice in my heart and the voice in my guts and that psychic voice in my mind, but Boobie couldn't hear me.

And I called out again and again and again till his hand fell and he started to fade, floating back and back and back, disappearing through the snowing trees.

After the Skylark ran out of gas, I took the TV and walked back to the van.

I kept thinking that if I dropped the TV the baby would fly off and disappear in all of that snow, so I stepped as careful as I could, one, two, three. I knew my Pro Flyers was all wack and worn down and smooth on the bottoms. I had to keep my frostbite hand over the baby's face so he wouldn't choke on no snow.

When we got back, the van was still snowing and the newspapers was flipping around and the frost was even whiter on the walls. It was so thick you could draw pictures in it with your finger.

For some reason I kept telling the baby not to be scared. I was like, "Don't be scared, baby. Don't be no little bitch. Ain't nothing gonna happen. Don't be scared." But the baby didn't seem scared at all. He was just staring up at me with them strange blue eyes and chewing on my frostbite hand with them little teeth that was starting to press through his gums.

Every time I looked at Curl I swear I thought I could see that heartbeat still going in her eye. I went over to her like four times and started shaking her, going, "Curl, Curl, wake up you dumb hooker!" But then I'd put my finger on her eye and feel that cold. And it wasn't cold like when a body gets cold. It was cold like when a *car* gets cold.

For a long time I just sat in the driver's seat with the baby and watched the snow. Just when you thought it would slow down, a bunch of it would start falling.

Every once in a while I'd see Curl through the windshield mirror. Her skin was so white it looked like glass. It was like she wasn't never no person. It was more like she was something that got made in a *factory,* like she was all stretched and blown and polished clean.

That little fish was still trapped in her cheek and her one froggy eye was staring out at them squiggles she spray-painted on the wall.

I put the TV down and walked over to Curl. I tried to pull her lid down but it was frozen so I took her one hand from over her head and put it over her eye.

When I flattened her hand you could feel how her fingers was all froze up like some dead sticks, and then that old wrinkled birthday card that she carried around fell out and it was all crumpled and small like Curl was trying to squeeze some life out of it. You could see her mom's writing and how her pen quit and how she had to get another one, cuz the colors of the ink changed.

I used the last diaper and changed the baby and fed him his last cup of bananas and his last box of milk. And I had to smash that box of milk and press it up against the wall of the van cuz it was frozen.

I took Curl's socks off and put them over the baby's hands. Then we got under the curtains and made a huddle. I used the curtain from the window, too. I put the baby under my puffy red coat cuz it was warmer that way. We stayed like that for a long time and just watched the night flying across the windows.

SELDOM

CUSTIS

I hear scratching at the front door. I got the baby curled up next to me so we can make a huddle and use the heat from each other's blood to keep warm.

We've been here like this all night and my stomach feels all small and shriveled, like there ain't nothing inside it but a old rusty penny.

So much snow has blown through the windows it's like we ain't even in the van. It's more like we're under one of them old trees outside.

Me and the baby is making a good huddle, though. Our breath is still smoking, which is good cuz that means our blood is hot enough to make us live.

At first I think the scratching is that big black turkey Curl kept talking about, like it's rubbing up against the door with one of its long, skinny turkey toes.

For some reason I look over at Curl again. I ain't been looking at her as much cuz for some reason it just makes me hungrier. I think it's cuz of the way her arms is all stretched out and skinny and how naked she is and how her little titties is all swollen and pointy like they never growed right. It's like her bones got longer since she died. Like God and Jesus and the devil himself pulled everything they could get out of them.

And even though she's dead I'm like, "Hey, Curl, that turkey's here. Should I let him in?"

Her skin is even whiter and her hands are turning kinda blue and there's frost on her eyelashes. She looks like some little wack granny.

I go, "Should I give that turkey your heart, Curl?" and I say all that shit out loud, too, like them homeless, bummy suckers from Renfro Park get when they start talking to the bushes.

Then I hear Curl's voice go, *Open the door, Custis. I ain't afraid of no big black turkey. Not no more.*

So I get out from under the curtains. It's so cold it's like I'm walking in a giant refrigerator. I put the baby under Curl's sunflower dress and then there's a knock at the door, but it ain't no scratching this time, and it don't sound like no turkey toe.

It's the kind of knocking that knuckles make.

And there it is again, going *tat-tat-tat.*

126

And now I'm walking toward the door all slow, and I can feel the baby's heart beating on my chest like a toy with a motor in it, and I step over the stop sign table and I step past the driver's seat and I reach my frostbite hand out toward the lever for the door and then there's that knocking again, *tat-tat-tat,* and I can see my frostbite hand shaking and I can see the veins in it curling like little blue snakes and I can see the black crawling on my fingers, and then I feel that metal lever in my hand and it's so cold it's like I can taste it in my teeth, and I pull it and the door creaks open and a bunch of snow flies in my face and just for a second I think if it ain't that big black turkey with the umbrella wings coming for Curl's heart then maybe it's *Boobie,* but when I open my eyes it ain't the big black turkey and it ain't Boobie neither. It's that old creaky nigger who made me clean his yard and he's standing on top of the snow like a giant and he's wearing this big old raincoat and he's wearing tennis rackets on his feet, and behind him that blue light from the moon makes him look blacker than a house that gets burnt down and he's just staring at me with his white eyes, and he's leaning on a long knobby stick, going, "Oh, my gracious light. Oh, my gracious light. . . ."

THE ITTY BITTY FARM

USTIS

The old nigger's name is Seldom and he's been living on the Itty Bitty Farm for *forty-some years*, so he says. In the backyard there's a old burnt-looking forest. And them trees look *superblack* cuz of how white the snow is.

Sometimes you can see animals running between the trees, like rabbits and foxes and these little things that look like smashed cats.

Seldom moves around the house real slow and he's got to crouch low so he don't hit his head in the door-ways. He says a hump started growing in his back cuz of crouching all them years, but he says he'd rather have a hump in his back from crouching than standing up straight and not having no house.

He's gotta stop a lot and hold his side, too, cuz he says he got kicked by a mule when he worked on his pops's farm in North Carolina when he was a kid. And even though his back got busted he says he fought in like forty-seven wars and shit. He said most of them wars didn't have nothing to do with no army or no other country or nothing like that. He said most of them wars was about his property and how the highway people was trying to run him off of it so they could build a two-lane road right through his living room.

Seldom always rubs his shins, too, and he says a lot of shit I don't understand like, "Good Godfrey," and "Watch your buttons," and wack stuff like that. I think he's like skeighty-eight years old or some shit but he won't tell me his age cuz I won't tell him my name.

Bob Motley says if you tell a nigger your name that he'll steal it and use it if he gets busted by the pigs, and he says that if that happens *you'll* be the one stuck making license plates in the penitentiary.

So at first Seldom called me Mr. Nowhere, but now he calls me Jimster and he calls the baby Little Jimster and I call him Seldom but I still don't know how old his lopsided ass is. But that's cool with me. The last thing I need is for him to get busted fucking a dog or some shit and then give the pigs *my* name. Bob Motley says that all niggers fuck dogs and sheep and that their dicks got hooks on the end.

Me and the baby sleep under the kitchen table cuz that bed in the extra room is so big I kept waking up feeling like I was falling off a cliff and shit. And there ain't nothing else in there but this old creaky baby crib that's got a bunch of old coats stacked in it. Seldom wanted to put the baby in it, but I was like, "You ain't puttin' him in that old skanky thing!"

So now Seldom lets us sleep under the kitchen table. The floor's old and sometimes you wake up with splinters in your hands, but it ain't too wack. It's better than looking at that old spooky baby crib, that's for sure.

Me and the baby was gonna try sleeping in the chicken coop cuz it had a good corner to sleepstand in, but Deuce — that wack little chicken I tried to steal — kept staring at me with its doll's eye, and Seldom kept laughing and telling me Deuce would just peck a bunch of holes in my clothes and that I wouldn't never got no sleep no ways.

It's easier for me to sleep *under* shit anyways.

Seldom gave us some blankets that smell like the fireplace and he gave us a couple of old skanky pillows, so it ain't really wack at all. And the tablecloth hangs down kinda low so it stays dark. The baby just sleeps in the TV cuz he's used to it. Every time Seldom tries taking him out and putting him on the floor he starts crying.

I like counting all the lines in wood on the bottom of the table. Curl used to say you can tell how old trees is by counting them lines.

When we first got here Seldom made me a big plate of mashed potatoes and gravy and I swallowed it so fast I almost got a migration headache. I kept giving my plate back and he just laughed and heaped on more. I had so much food in my mouth I could hardly breathe. My stomach got so full you could almost hear it stretching.

Seldom gave the baby some smashed pinto beans cuz he said he needed protein, and I showed him how to feed him with the back of your thumb. At first I wasn't so sure about that long, bony, nigger thumb going into the baby's mouth, but I guess the way Seldom kept smiling and laughing made it seem cool.

When I was finished with them mashed potatoes Seldom asked me to put my dishes in the sink and I did and then we took a big metal garbage can out back and started a fire to melt the snow and make the ground soft. He kept rolling the can around and before you knew it you could see the grass. It was all brown and hard-looking. Bob Motley would've been surprised, seeing a old creaky nigger being smart like that.

Then Seldom went inside and came back out holding two shovels and he handed me the smaller one and we starting digging this deep hole, like so deep you could *disappear* in it and shit. And we was all slipping and trying to not-slip, and my frostbite hand kept catching cramps, and some of that dirt didn't get softened by the fire and it was hard to go deeper and we had to keep at it with our shovels, but we did it.

You could hear Seldom breathing them long, slow nigger breaths and you could smell how old he was cuz his breath smelled like leather shoes and dirt, and he had to stop a bunch of times to hold his side and rub his shins and go, "Good Godfrey," and "This durn old back," and shit.

I had to stop a couple of times to check on the baby. Once I had to change his diaper and give him some warm milk. Seldom showed me how to throw some milk in a pan and light the stove so I didn't have to ask him to help me every time the baby started crying.

Whenever we stopped digging we sort of stared at them flames sawing in the garbage can, and it was like the flames got inside of us, like they warmed up some vitamins in our bones and gave us energy to finish making the hole.

At the end we was all wet and folded over, but we eventually got it dug.

Then Seldom pulled out this big jug of water and we drank it down, and it tasted sweet like it had sugar in it and all you could hear was our breath slowing down, and after we rested for a few minutes, he gave me a pair of tennis rackets and strapped them to my Pro Flyers and we walked back to the van through the snow with this big burlap sack.

The sky was all gray and wack-looking and it was hard walking on top of all that snow, but I started to get the hang of it. It was like we was walking to the North Pole and shit.

When we got to the van Curl was all white and blue and glassy-looking. That little fish even looked glassy on her cheek.

We had to push her arms down and they was real stiff. And they wasn't just stiff the way clothes get stiff when you leave them on the laundry line. Them arms was stiff the way a *table* is stiff.

While Seldom was fitting Curl in the sack I found Boobie's book. It was wedged next to the driver's seat. I held it in my hands and just stared at it for a minute. I was gonna open it but I couldn't do it. I don't even know why. Something about it just felt all wack, so I stuck it under my puffy red coat.

We carried Curl back to the Itty Bitty Farm. She was pretty heavy cuz of them death juices but we managed it pretty crisp.

When we was carrying her it wasn't like we was really carrying Curl. It was more like we was carrying a big sack of rocks or potatoes or some shit.

I tried picturing her in the sack, but I couldn't see her face. I couldn't see her nose or her lips or that froggy heartbeat and how it froze in her eye. I couldn't even picture her arms or her legs. I could only see them rocks and potatoes.

Me and Seldom didn't say nothing to each other the whole time. He had to walk real slow cuz of his side and his shins. I just kept moving and concentrated on lifting them tennis rackets over the snow.

The sky was going darker and that purple started creeping over them dirty clouds. For a second I wondered if Boobie was staring up at the sky, too. I wondered if he was warm and had enough food.

When we got back to the Itty Bitty Farm we put the sack in the hole and we pushed all the dirt back in and packed it down hard with our shovels. Then we both just kinda fell down and sat on top of it for a while.

Seldom took this little Bible out of his pocket and started saying some of these wack prayers and I just kinda looked off and stared at the sky.

It took a while for him to say them prayers and I don't think he could read too good or maybe them words was real big and shit, cuz he had to stop a lot and put his finger in the Bible like he was squashing bugs.

Even though Seldom kept saying them prayers, I thought maybe God wouldn't let Curl into heaven cuz he's such a sucker; like she would walk up to that check-in station or that holy tollbooth, and some angel with big black boots would come out and kick her in the ass and throw her off the cloud.

And I thought about Boobie again and how they probably wouldn't even let him on the cloud cuz of what he done to his parents, how they would just throw a bunch of lightning and shit at him.

When Seldom was finished he put the Bible back in his pocket and rubbed his shins and we just sat there and stared at the sky for a while. Seldom kept shaking his head all long and slow.

He went, "You was friends?"

I nodded.

Then he patted some of the dirt and went, "How old was she?"

"Fourteen, I think. Maybe fifteen."

"Shucks."

I just sat there for a minute. That purple light was covering the sky like a big greasy blanket.

Seldom went, "That's too durn young," and wiped some sweat off his head with a rag and went, "Shuckaloo shucks," whatever that means.

For some reason I was like, "She wasn't shit but a two-dollar hooker."

"She was?"

"She'd do any man with a pair of shoes."

"That's shameful."

I was like, "Chump change or food stamps, it didn't matter."

Seldom wiped his face again and went, "She prolly didn't know no better."

And I was like, "She didn't know shit."

Then we was quiet again and Seldom looked off like some old scratchy song was playing in his head.

Then he went, "Lost my wife thirty years ago this past May."

I didn't know what to say when he said that shit, so I just stayed quiet.

Seldom poked in the dirt again and went, "Lost her giving birth to our baby. Died right when that little thing started coming out. Baby died, too. Little girl. The 'bilical string was wrapped around her neck. Came out blue. Eyes didn't even have no color in them. Poor thing never had a chance."

Then Seldom drawed something in the dirt with his finger and pointed over at this small, wack shed that looked like something a dog might live in. When I looked in the dirt to check out what he drawed there wasn't nothing to see.

Then he went, "Buried both of them right over there."

I looked to where he was pointing. There were two small crosses that looked more like something you hang socks on than something you'd see in a bone yard.

Seldom's eyes turned kinda cloudy for a second. Even under all that purple sky you could see how they went cloudy. He rubbed his shins and kind of rocked back and forth like that memory he had was too strong for his old creaky body.

In the distance you could hear a train whistle. It sounded like it was a million miles away.

Seldom went, "What was your friend's name?"

I almost didn't tell him cuz of that shit Bob Motley

says about niggers stealing names. But for some reason I did anyways. I got a picture of her in my head and went, "Curl."

"Was she Little Jimster's mama?"

"She just took care of him. Fed him and changed his diapers and shit."

"Well, she did okay."

"She didn't even like him."

Then Seldom shook his head some more and said, "God's gravy, God's gravy," or maybe he said, "God's gray, God's gray," I couldn't tell for sure. Sometimes his words come out like he's got a bunch of gum in his mouth. I think it's cuz of them fake lower teeth he wears.

Then Seldom went, "You love the mess outta that boy, don't you?"

I was like, "He's all right."

"Little Jimster with them cornflower eyes. . . . You love him and you loved her, too."

I just nodded and tried to go, "She was like my sister," but it didn't really come out cuz it was all stuck in my throat like a hunk of meat.

Then I started crying like a little bitch. I don't know why. I wasn't feeling nothing the whole time we was digging that hole and walking through the snow — nothing but cold and numb and tired. But all of the sudden, sitting on that dirt with Seldom and holding that shovel, that hot, thick feeling was flying up my throat and the next thing I knew my face was all wet.

I was like, "Goddamn hooker. Goddamn bazooka-fiending hooker."

Then Seldom put his big old hand right on my head and I didn't even care. Sometimes Sister Blister would do that shit, too. It was the only thing that that wack spelling nun did to me that I liked halfway.

After a minute Seldom went, "You believe in God, Jimster?"

I was like, "God ain't shit."

"Watch yourself, now."

"He don't care."

"He do, though. He just don't show it sometimes."

"He ain't shown me nothin'."

"He will. He will. You just gotta have faith."

Then for some reason I was like, "He's prolly just some old creaky garbage man who smells like gasoline."

Seldom started laughing that old scratchy laugh, and went, "Good Godfrey, Jimster. Good Godfrey." Then he took his hand off my head and started rubbing his shins and went, "The things you say . . ."

I just sat there all quiet and wiped my face. Seldom put his hand back on my head for a minute and even patted it a few times. He patted my head like I was a dog, and that shit felt pretty good.

Then he went, "Well, I best go get that tree."

I was like, "What tree?"

He went, "That tree over yonder," and waved his hand at this big pointy tree leaning against the other side of the shed. There was all these old shingles curling off the shed and it made the tree look kind of wack and skanky.

I went, "You gonna burn it?"

He was like, "Burn it!? I'm gonna drag that old lady in the house and throw popcorn at her!"

"How come?"

"Don't you know what day it is, Jimster?"

I was like, "No." And I didn't know, either. I didn't know shit.

"It's Christmas Eve!"

Then Seldom starting laughing again and you could see his teeth shining. Even though the sky was way darker than purple now, you could see them.

That's when I got up and went in the house to check on the baby.

When I reached the door I looked back where we buried Curl. Seldom just stayed right there. He had that Bible out again and he was using his finger to read one of them other prayers. His face looked real old and sad. Even though he was still smiling with them shiny teeth, it looked like that.

The way his head was bowed looked kinda nice.

So that night Seldom stood the tree up in the living room and popped popcorn and we did what he called a "Christmas throw."

He threw all wack and left-handed like the bone in

his arm was weak. He kept calling the tree the "old lady," and he was dancing all over the room and pumping his fist and cheering me on and shit.

I hit the tree like skeighty-eight times, from every part of the living room; from behind his couch; from both sides of the fireplace; even from the doorway to the bathroom.

In the window you could see the snow falling again, but it wasn't going sideways no more. It was just falling regular.

Seldom kept clapping his hands, going, "Throw that popcorn, Jimster! Hit that old lady. Throw it like you know it!" And I *did* know it, too. I threw that shit the way me and Boobie used to throw rocks at the buses in Rockdale.

Seldom almost fell down a few times cuz he was dancing so much. Once he sat right in the fireplace and almost burnt his old bow-legged ass. He had to rest after that cuz he said his *sticks* was hurting, but he kept clapping his hands and cheering me on from his rocking chair.

After we finished the Christmas throw, Seldom let Deuce come inside to eat the popcorns that didn't stick to the tree. I swear, that little wack chicken was walking around just like a person, and it stared at me the whole time with that freaky doll's eye.

There ain't no TV or no radio or no PlayStation II on the Itty Bitty Farm. It was just the fire and the Christmas tree and whatever light you could see coming through the window. I brought the baby's TV in so the baby could have Christmas, too. All three of us just sat there in front of the fire kinda quiet and still. It took Seldom a while to catch his breath. You could hear his lung bubbles fighting for that Itty Bitty Farm air.

I ain't never sat in front of no Christmas fire before, so it was pretty crisp. In the window you could see the snow falling and the reflection of the Christmas tree and how all the popcorn stuck. And you could see the flames from the fireplace sawing up and making shit kinda glow. In that reflection sometimes you couldn't tell what was the snow and what was popcorn, and that was pretty crisp, too.

The reflection in the window made it feel like there was *two* Christmas trees and shit.

Seldom creaked back and forth in his rocking chair with his long bony shins looking all dry and brown like some old rope, and I dropped my frostbite hand in the TV and let the baby chew on it.

Seldom went, "This ain't so bad, is it, Jimster?"

I was like, "It's okay."

"Just okay?"

"It ain't like no Halloween parade."

Then he went, "Boy . . ."

And I was like, "Boy what?"

He went, "You sure are tough to please," and creaked this big long rock in the rocking chair. "Still got that hard shoulder."

I was like, "No I don't," and just stared at that reflection of the Christmas tree in the window. We didn't say nothing for like five minutes. All you could hear was that rocking chair creaking all ancient and wack like it was a car breaking down or some shit.

Then Seldom looked at me and went, "Look at you."

I was like, "What?"

"Ornery like you old."

"I ain't ornery."

"You don't like nothin'."

"Yes I do."

"Why you so hateful? You don't even like the tree."

I went, "I like it."

"What do you like about it?"

I went, ". . . Like *like* like?"

"No like like *hate*. Whatchu think?"

Then we didn't say nothing again for a minute and I didn't know it but I was eating some popcorn right off the floor, and it was that skanky shit that Deuce wouldn't even touch. It didn't taste wack or nothing, though.

Seldom went, "Well?"

I was like, "Well what?"

"What do you like? About the tree?"

I went, "*Seriously?*"

Then Seldom made this face like he was mad. He wouldn't even look at me. I tried spying on him through

145

the reflection in the window, but I could only see one of his big long legs.

I went, "I like it."

"*Shoo.*"

I was like, "I do."

"You can't even say one thing about it. Nary a thing."

Then I felt like I had a fist all clenched up in my stomach. I couldn't say nothing for like two whole minutes, but I took a deep breath and went, "I like the way the popcorn's all like . . . spread out and shit."

Seldom went, "Spread out how?"

"How it looks . . ."

"How it looks what?"

"Like how it looks kinda like stars, okay? Damn."

We was quiet for a minute. Then he went, "*Shoo,*" again. I think that's like Seldom's favorite shit to say. You could say, "Hey, Seldom, there's some gum on your toe!" and he'd just go, "*Shoo.*" Or you could be like, "Hey, Seldom, the sky is falling!" or "Hey, Seldom, there's a hooker on a pogo stick and she's flashing her pussy!" and he would just look at you with them big white eyes and go, "*Shoo.*"

You could hear the fire hissing and Seldom creaking in the rocking chair.

Then he shook his head and went, "One is a lonely number, Jimster," but I didn't know what that shit meant so I didn't say nothing back. I just ate some more popcorn and what I didn't eat I threw into the fireplace and listened to those flames make it pop.

He went, "You know what I like about it?"

I went, "No."

Then he started talking real fast, like someone flipped a switch on his back or some shit.

He said, "I like *everything* about it. I like the way it smells and I like how tall it is and I like how some of the needles already gone and fell to the floor and I like how she kind of leans to the left a little like she's thinkin' about something and I like how you was throwing the popcorn. . . ." Then he said that first part again. He went, "I like *everything* about it, Jimster, okay?" and looked away.

For some reason I told him to stop being a little bitch. I was like, "Stop being a little bitch, Seldom."

Seldom looked at me like he was a little kid, I swear, with his eyes all big and wide and white and his mouth kinda open like when some gum falls out and you don't got none left. He looked at me like that and went, "I ain't being no little bitch."

I went, "Little Christmas bitch," and he kept hanging his mouth open and tried to swallow something but there wasn't nothing in there to swallow. I just stared into the fire.

After a minute Seldom went, "You hurt my feelings, Jimster. You must like hurting my feelings. It's like you don't appreciate nothin'."

I was like, "I 'preciate stuff."

"You can't even think of one more nice thing to say about the tree."

"Yes I can."

"Bet you can't."

"How much?"

"I'll bet you a nickel."

"I don't got no nickel."

"I'll spot you."

"Cool."

I couldn't think of nothing right away like that, but that nickel was on the line.

Seldom went, "So go on then. Say it. One more thing."

I was like, "I will, okay?"

Then Seldom got that look on his face again and went, "And somethin' nice, durn it!"

Part of me didn't want to say *shit* after all that bitching he was doing. But I thought hard for a minute and then I was like, "Okay."

"Okay what."

"I got something for your old creaky ass."

"This old creaky ass'll still smack the tailbone right out your backside, you don't watch it."

"You gonna owe me a nickel."

"Shoo."

"I can already feel it in my pocket."

"Well, go on then!"

So I did. I went, "I like the way it smells."

Seldom went, "I already said that."

"No you didn't."

"Yes I did. I said I likeded how it smelled and I said how I likeded how tall it is and I said how I likeded how some of the needles done already gone and fell to the floor and I said how I likeded how she kind of leans to the left a little like she's thinkin' about something and I said how I likeded how you was throwing the popcorn. You owe me a nickel. *Shoo*."

Then for some reason I went, "Likeded ain't no word," cuz I remember how them spelling nuns was slapping their pointers on the blackboard cuz I used it wrong once. I was supposed to put it in a sentence and go to the front of the class and say that shit out loud to the rest of the retards, and I tried saying I likeded Nerds and chocolate milk and them nuns started slapping their pointers up against the blackboard and popping off about how I wasn't *improving* and shit, and then later on Sister Blister came over to me all hush hush and made me write, "I liked the Nerds and the chocolate milk," correctly like skeighty-eight times, and she made me underline *liked* so I wouldn't mess it up no more. I think that's why I said that shit to Seldom.

Seldom just looked at me with that little kid face again and went, "Likeded's a goddog word."

I was like, "No it ain't."

"Is too."

"Is not."

"*Shoo . . .*"

Then I looked over at Seldom and he was staring right in my eyes, still waiting for me to come up with something else about the Christmas tree, and let me tell you, when that old nigger wants to stare at you, he'll do it so hard you think you can hear the *blood* floating in your veins and shit, so I went, "I like how . . ."

"Yeah?"

"I like how——"

"Easter's comin'."

I was like, "Damn, Seldom, let me say the shit!"

"Well, go 'head and say it then. Quit stallin'!"

I waited for him to start rocking again and then I went, "I like how the reflection looks . . . in the window," and I said it kind of slow cuz for some reason that shit was like almost *impossible* to say.

Seldom went, "What about it?"

"I like it cuz . . . it's like there's two trees. Like it's double, okay? *Damn!*"

Then we was quiet again. I swear, for some reason, saying that shit was like pulling a *bone* out of my stomach.

After a minute, Seldom went, "You ain't never had no tree, have you?"

I was like, "I had a tree."

"When?"

"I had one."

"Shoo."

"One night when I stayed at this juvy hotel in Franklin Park. They had a tree there. Right where you signed the book."

"Right where you signed the book? You sure?"

"Yeah, it was blue."

"A blue tree?"

"It was fake."

"Good Godfrey."

"I liked it."

"Prolly smelled like a furniture store."

"I slept under it."

"You did?"

"Right on the snow."

Seldom waited a few seconds after that and went, "I 'spose the snow was blue, too."

I was like, *"It was white."*

Then we didn't say nothing and I threw the last few pieces of popcorn into the fire. After they popped I felt like talking for some reason, so I went, "I couldn't never sleep in them wack beds they had."

"Why not?"

"I don't know."

Seldom went, "I know why."

And even though I knew it was a trap, I was like, "Why?"

Then he went, "Cuz you so ornery."

"I ain't ornery."

"Ornery as a bowl fulla bees."

"I just ain't used to sleeping in no bed, okay?"

Then Seldom was quiet for a minute. You could hear the rocking chair creaking. He didn't seem like he was gonna say nothing so I kept going.

I went, "Them beds at them Rockdale juvy hotels is too skinny, anyways. Felt like you was laying in a coffin and shit."

Seldom didn't say nothing about that. Instead he went, "You slept all night under a blue Christmas tree?"

"Till the security pig kicked me out."

"Why'd he kick you out?"

"Cuz he caught me trying to steal some presents."

"Jimster."

"Wasn't shit in 'em 'cept for some Styrofoam."

"Good Godfrey."

"And peanuts. You'd think them juvy hotel people would give a kid more than some Styrofoam peanuts. That place was wack, anyways."

"You a character."

"*You* a character."

"Crazy Jimster."

"Crazy Seldom."

Then Seldom made this face like he *was* crazy, with his long pink tongue flopping out of his mouth like some half-cooked fish and his big white eyes popping.

On top of that, he flipped his bottom teeth out at me and that shit made me laugh.

Seldom went, "Got you to smile."

I was like, "I ain't smiling," but I was smiling so hard I could feel it in my feet and shit.

"Don't do it too much you might hurt yourself."

I tried to stop but I couldn't. It felt like feathers was flying through my body, from the top of my head all the way down to my toes. I laughed like that for like two minutes, and those two minutes felt all loose and jangly, cuz it was like the three of us — me and Seldom and the baby — it was like the three of us was all warm from the fireplace and from throwing the popcorn at the tree and from just *being* there together and shit.

But then after a minute, for some reason I started *eating* that laughter, and about halfway through eating it I started crying. I don't know why. And it wasn't just no normal little-bitch cry; that shit felt like it was coming out of my *feet* and my *ass* and the *bones in my back*.

Then, the next thing I knew, I was walking over to Seldom where he was rocking in his rocking chair. It was like my legs was going on their own, one, two, three. And then I was like on my knees and shit and hugging his long bony shins. And I cried into his legs for a long time and he just sat there and rocked away, going, "It's okay, Jimster. It's gonna be okay." And he said it like skeighty-eight times with his old scratchy voice.

The fire smelled all thick and sweet and that reflection of the Christmas tree was kinda shining in the window and you could see the snow falling through it.

I'll never forget how good them long bony shins felt in my arms. And I'll never forget the sound of that rocking chair creaking back and forth. And I'll never forget how Seldom's hand was like a big warm hat holding my head together.

BOOBIE

CUSTIS

I'm in the bathroom sitting on the toilet. The water's going in the shower and there's so much steam it's like I'm in a cloud. I like getting the steam up in the bathroom so I can make Pigmy feet on the mirror.

All of the sudden the door opens and Seldom's standing there, ducking his head in.

He goes, "Hey, Jimster."

I'm like, "Hey what?"

"How come you don't never wash yourself?"

I go, "I do."

Then he goes, "No you don't. You turn the water

on but you don't never get in. You just sit there on the toilet like you doin' now."

"I get in."

"No you don't."

I'm like, "Shows what you know."

Then Seldom says, "You don't got no reason to lie to me."

"I ain't lyin'."

"You know the door don't close all the way. I see you sittin' there like that every time. Either sittin' there or playin' that game on the mirror. What's that game you always playin', anyway?"

I go, "I ain't playin' no game."

He waves some steam away from his face and goes, "Wastin' all that water. What kinda sense is that?"

I go, "You waste more water than me."

"Shoo."

I go, "You gotta use more water to clean them old skanky bones."

"The only thing I'm wastin is my time tryin' to talk some sense into you."

Then I don't say nothing. I just stick my hand under the water and flick it at him. He ducks all low like I'm throwing rocks at him or some shit.

He goes, "Stop, now," and starts reaching out for this little wack-looking towel that he keeps over the sink. He finally grabs it and wipes his face, and he wipes that shit a lot longer than he has to.

Then he goes, "And you smell terrible."

I go, "*You* smell terrible."

"You need to take some soap and water to your dirty self."

"I don't need to do shit."

"Fine. Suit yourself. I'm just trying to help you."

I'm like, "I don't need no help."

He says, "You sure don't, do you. You don't never need nothin' from no one."

Now the steam is going out into the house and he's waving at it like it's a bunch of mosquitoes or some shit.

"I put them extra washcloths in there and everything for you, too," he says, still waving at that steam.

Then I flick some more water at him and he takes these big long bow-legged steps across the bathroom and reaches into the shower and turns the water off.

"Ain't no one gonna like bein' around you, smellin' like you do. That's why Deuce don't like you."

I go, "Can't I get no privacy? What do you care what I'm doin' in here?"

He just stands there looking at them Pigmy feet I made on the mirror. For a minute I think he might reach out and touch one, but instead of touching one he goes, "And why don't you never wash your hair? I bought you that fancy shampoo and everything. That dippity-doo stuff that smells like soda pop."

I just look at him staring at them Pigmy feet and go, "Wash your own hair." Then I go, "Oh yeah, you don't got none."

He goes, "Ha ha, very funny."

And I'm like, "Ha ha, very funny," right back at him.

"So funny I forgot my keys."

I say, "That don't even make no sense."

"Forgot my keys and forgot my knees. Trees, bees, and a truckloada fleas."

It usually makes me laugh when he says that crazy shit, but I hide it pretty good. I feel like I pretty much got his ass beat this time.

But then Seldom comes real close and looks at me and sees how my face is starting to lift cuz of that stuff he said about the trees and the bees and the fleas living in that truck, so he reaches down real quick — and that old nigger can get quick when he wants to — he reaches down and sticks his thumbs in my ribs. Whenever he does that I can't help but laugh cuz of how long and bony them old creaky thumbs are. When I jump he lifts the toilet seat and holds it up and stares into the bowl like he's staring at a dead rat.

Then he lowers the seat and goes, "And flush the durn toilet, Jimster. I don't want to be always walkin' in on your slops like that."

I go, "*You* flush the dang toilet."

Then he goes, "I didn't say dang I said durn," and he says it all quick like he won.

I just go, "*Durn* toilet. Whatever."

Then he thumbs me in the ribs again and I laugh and a little green booger flies out of my nose and sticks to my shirt.

Now Seldom's laughing, too. And he's laughing so hard he's gotta lean up against the sink so he won't fall in the shower.

He goes, "You a piece of work, Jimster," and then he reaches over and flushes the toilet. "A real piece of work."

The night after we took the tree down and dragged it out back next to the shed I woke up under the kitchen table all strange and wack-feeling.

The baby was sleeping real good and the moonlight from the kitchen window was reaching into the TV and laying on his face all soft and blue and quiet. It was so blue it even made the seam in his forehead look kinda blue.

I crawled out from under the kitchen table and walked into Seldom's room. It was cold and I was kinda shivering and you could feel the air from the basement coming through the cracks in the floor. I had them astronaut legs and it felt like I was walking in a time warp and shit.

Through the living room window I could see the Christmas tree laying next to the shed. It was all sad and wack-looking, like somebody shot it with a *gat* or some shit. There was still some popcorn stuck in the branches.

I had to open the door to Seldom's room real quiet, cuz it squeaks like them old creaky shinbones in his legs.

There ain't shit in his room but his big old bed that looks like a boat and this wooden box that he keeps near the bed. He always keeps half of his teeth soaking in a glass of water, and next to the glass is this picture of him and his wife from when they was married. It's black-and-white like them pictures you see in newspapers and it's got a date on the frame. I can't do the math right but you can tell that that shit is like skeighty-eight years old cuz the corners is all skanked and yellow.

In the picture Seldom don't have none of them old wrinkles on his forehead and he's got hair and his smile is so big it's like half the moon shining in the middle of his face.

His wife's got these big juicy lips and she's real pretty for a nigger woman. Their heads are kinda touching like they got the same thought; like they got that psychic love thing going and shit.

Seldom was asleep and his face was all black and burnt-looking. His mouth was kind of open and his bottom teeth was missing. But his top teeth was so white they looked like that shit the toilet factories use.

You could hear the air sliding in and out of his lung bubbles, going *sloosh-sloosh-sloosh,* and you could see his one eye twitching a little.

The moon looked all swollen in the window, and that same blue light that was laying on the baby's face was laying across Seldom's, too.

He almost looked like he was dead with them bottom

teeth missing and that moonlight on his face. I just stood there and watched him sleep for a minute.

When he woke up his nose twitched a little and he just laid there and stared at me.

"What you doin', Jimster?"

I didn't say nothing back. I just took my pants down and climbed up in his bed. His mattress is real high off the floor so you kind of have to jump up in it.

After I got up in his bed I turned away from him and got on my hands and knees like a dog.

I didn't notice it when I walked in the room, but on the wall across from his bed there was a picture of this clown with balloons in his cheeks. The clown had this upside-down smile and he looked sad and happy at the same time. I just stared at the picture and waited for Seldom to do what I knew he was going to do.

Seldom went, "Jimster?" again, but I just stayed there like that for a minute. I just stayed there all doggy-style and naked with my ass in the air.

Seldom went, *"You asleep, Jimster?"*

I just went, "Go 'head, Seldom. Go on and do me."

Then I closed my eyes tight and I held my breath cuz I knew he had his big nigger dick out and I knew it was all long and scabby and I knew it had that hook on the end of it like Bob Motley talked about.

And I just knew that shit was going to *hurt* when he stuck it in me and took my buns, too. It didn't matter how much hair grease or motor oil he used. But I didn't care. I just said it again.

I went, "Go on and fuck me."

But Seldom didn't do *shit*. He just grabbed me and turned me around real fast and slapped me across my face and it stung like some bees and then the next thing I know he's sliding my pants back over my feet and over my legs and over my ass, and he's sliding them so fast they burn my knees, and then he zips up the zipper and snaps the front snap and takes his big hand and puts it on my face and wipes these hot tears off my cheeks.

"I ain't gonna do that to you, Jimster," he said, kinda shaking my shoulders. "That ain't me."

I felt real small all of the sudden. Smaller than I ever felt in my life. Like I was turning into a plastic toy or some shit.

Then Seldom went, "And what's wrong with your fanny? You got all types of stuff. . . ."

I got out of Seldom's bed real slow and just sat on the floor. For some reason it felt better down there.

I did a thirty-three even though I hadn't done one in a long time.

My face was wet where he slapped me. I could almost feel his big-ass hand still on my skin and how the heat from it sunk way deep into my teeth and into the bones in my jaw.

I could feel him watching me and I could feel how he was all frozen and scared, so I just kept doing that thirty-three and let them numbers make shit slow down.

After my thirty-three I got even lower and just laid on the floor. I spread my arms and my legs as wide as they could go and just let the magnets in the earth hold me there like that.

My heart felt all sick and small in my chest.

After a while Seldom lowered one of his pillows and lifted my head and slid the pillow under the bend in my neck.

I started another thirty-three. *One, two, three . . .*

The last thing I remember is staring at that picture of the clown with the balloons in its cheeks.

CUSTIS

The next day, Seldom walked into town with them tennis rackets stuck to his shoes and came back with these little penicillin pills. I had to take them three times a day, and drinking all that water kept making me fart, but it didn't hurt no more when I shit, and I started taking showers, too, cuz I didn't have to worry about that burning.

That shampoo Seldom got me did smell like pop, too. Like some cherry cola or some shit. I even started combing my hair. I tried to do it like Boobie's, with a part down the middle.

Things was pretty crisp after that.

Me and Seldom got real good at living together.

In the mornings, he would wake up early and feed Deuce, and I would feed the baby and change his diaper in the bathroom.

Then I'd sweep the floor and take the trash out to the backyard and burn it and watch the smoke curl over the Itty Bitty Farm all black and skanky.

The snow kept coming and Seldom kept watching it through the window, shaking his head, going, "My gracious light. Oh, my gracious light." Sometimes it came down sideways, but most of the time it just came from everywhere.

We even had to shovel our way out of the house a few times. That was kinda fun, though, like we was at the North Pole and shit.

Seldom gave me a pair of old gloves and this long-ass yellow scarf that I had to wrap around my neck like skeighty-eight times just so I wouldn't trip over it.

Seldom also gave me this crazy hat that looked like a cinnamon roll.

I got pretty crisp at walking with them tennis rackets. You gotta lift and go slow. Seldom always said, "Go slow and know the snow."

We kept the Christmas tree in the backyard for a long time. And even though it started turning all brown and skanky, it was still cool to look through the window and see it laying next to the shed.

Every once in a while Deuce would come into the living room walking like one of them Bolingbrook hookers. Seldom would pop popcorn and throw it on the floor and talk to her the way you talk to someone on the telephone. Deuce would just start eating the popcorn and walk right back out, burning a stare through me with that doll's eye the whole time.

Sometimes it seemed like she didn't even have to wait for Seldom to come get her from the chicken coop. It was like she could just *appear;* like she had special *powers* and shit.

At night we'd build fires and just sit there in the living room. Sometimes you could hear that train whistle off in the distance. That was about the loneliest sound in the world. Sometimes I pictured me and the baby on that train. But in the picture we was always cold and shivering and starving to death and both of us had lung frosts.

But then Seldom would kinda hum like he was remembering something, and that lonely train feeling would go away.

I think my time on the Itty Bitty Farm's been some of the best days I've ever had. Even better than when me and Boobie and Curl was living back in the woods.

There's always plenty of food to eat and there ain't never no driving and you always wake up in the same place every morning. Even if it's under a kitchen table sometimes, it's still the same place.

I guess the Itty Bitty Farm became the most official crib I ever lived in.

And them migration headaches didn't come once.

Sometimes in the middle of the night me and the baby would creep into Seldom's room and sleep next to him on the floor. He started leaving one of his pillows and a extra blanket for us. I liked the smell of the pillow. It was kinda like a old coat that gets left in the closet.

After the morning chores we'd stick them tennis rackets to the bottom of our shoes and go looking for sticks together. It wasn't too easy cuz of all the snow, but I got used to it.

Seldom made a pouch for the baby out of a pillow-case. He poked four holes in it — two for my arms and two for the baby's legs; that way I could carry him on my back when we was stick collecting. The baby didn't give no shit. He would just squeak and wiggle and play with my ears.

At first I thought we was collecting sticks for fire-wood, but Seldom said he had enough firewood in the shed to last for like a year and shit. He said we was collecting sticks cuz we was gonna make a raft. I was like, "A *raft*?" and he was like, "Shoo, you'll see."

He said we needed a raft cuz one day the sun was going to come out burning like crazy, and he said it would burn so hot that all of the snow around the Itty Bitty Farm and all of the other snow over by the van and the Crow Wing River and all the snow from like skeighty-eight miles around was gonna melt all at once and start a flood and that the Itty Bitty Farm would just get drowned in it.

He said we was gonna build a raft big enough for me and him and the baby and Deuce. He said we was gonna have to build it on top of the house cuz once the snow started melting everything was gonna flood so fast we wasn't gonna have much time.

At first I thought he was crazy, but then I started looking at all the snow around the house and how it was higher than some of the windows. And I looked at how that shit was *still* coming down; how even though it wasn't sideways no more that it was *still* falling.

So we started putting all them sticks and tree branches on top of the roof and Seldom would stay up there for hours, joining them parts together with rope and twine and this skanky waterproof stuff that smelled terrible.

It even started to look like a real raft after a while, too; the way a raft looks if you see it on a cartoon or in a comic book or some shit.

Sometimes I would bring the baby up to the roof with me and all three of us would sit on the raft like we was practicing for the flood.

Seldom would tease Deuce and go, "Hey, Deucey, we leavin' without you. Watch your buttons," and shit like that. Deuce would just kind of peck at the roof and walk around in these funny little circles.

One day me and Seldom and the baby was all just sitting there on the roof, watching the sunset and how them colors was kind of melting through the sky. I had a big spool of twine between my legs and the baby was kind of pulling on it from his pillowcase when Seldom went, "Hey, Jimster, can I ask you somethin'?"

I just nodded and kept watching them colors falling through the sky.

He was like, "Who's Tiny?"

I was like, "Who?"

And he went, "Big Tiny."

I went, "Big *who*?"

"You heard me."

"I don't know no Big Tiny."

"You did last night. You was talkin' to her in your sleep."

"Sounds like you was trippin'."

"You was talkin' to her like she was layin right next to you on the floor. Goin' 'Yes, ma'am, yes ma'am, I promise.' Real quiet. Like you was whisperin' in her ear. You was dreamin'."

"*You* was dreamin'."

A few days later we was in the kitchen. Seldom was washing dishes and I was rolling pennies and watching the baby at the table.

The night before I creeped into his room and slept on his floor again and when I woke up, Seldom's bed was all made up and the sun was shining through the window and you could see the colors of the balloons in the cheeks from that clown picture, and you could see dust sliding in the light. My back was all sore from sleeping on that hard-ass floor.

When I came out to the kitchen Seldom had just got done feeding Deuce. He was whistling this song and wiping some dust off the shelf over the fireplace. He was in such a good mood I thought he was gonna fart balloons and shit.

Then he grabbed the baby out of the TV and started singing this old wack song about how nickels sound like rain when you got enough of them in your pocket and he was holding the baby over his head and kinda dancing with him and you could see the baby kinda smiling and you could see the muscles muscling around that seam in his forehead.

For some reason I started feeling that fist going hard in my stomach again, and all of the sudden I was like, "He ain't yours."

Seldom stopped and turned to me. He went, "I know he ain't mine, Jimster. But I can play with him, can't I?"

He was holding the baby in front of him now. The baby looked like the whitest baby in world. He looked like a *snow* baby and shit.

Then Seldom went, "He likes me," and turned the baby so he could look at him and went, "Don't you, Little Jimster?"

I just sat at the kitchen table for a minute and watched how that light was pouring in through the window. It was real bright that morning, like the sun was out for revenge or some shit. You could see dust sliding through the light in the kitchen, too.

Seldom shifted the baby to his other side like he'd been practicing that shit and went, "Come on now. I'm makin' pancakes."

But I still wouldn't move. I was getting pissed off for some reason and I think Seldom knew cuz of how I was all still.

Then Seldom went, "You can have him back," and held out the baby, and the way he was holding him made it look like the baby was going to fall and I pictured that old bone in Seldom's arm crumbling or breaking or some shit, so I got up and took the baby.

I didn't even look at Seldom.

I just went and sat back down at the table.

Then one day when we was picking sticks, out of nowhere, Seldom goes, "What about Scooby?"

"Huh?"

"Scooby."

I was like, "*Whooby?*"

"Last night you was talkin' in your sleep again. You You was goin' 'Run, Scooby, run!' and stuff like that."

It was kinda funny how Seldom was asking me all these questions but he wouldn't look at me. It was like he was trying to be slick and shit. Like he was one of them private investigator pigs you see on TV.

I just kept walking in the snow with them sticks I'd

picked. The baby was playing with my ears and I think he shit his pants cuz you could smell it.

Then, all of the sudden while we was walking in the snow, the dream I had from the night before came back to me:

I was in the backyard looking at the woods behind the Itty Bitty Farm. I was burning garbage and watching the smoke curl over the roof. Seldom was building the raft. Them woods looked all black and dead and skanked and then all of the sudden *Boobie* came out of the trees and just stood there looking at me. His hair was white like the snow and he just stood there with his hands in his pockets. That white hair made his eyes look blacker than ever. I could feel his stare inside of me pretty crisp, but he didn't say nothing, he just stood there. And for some reason, with my dream mind I had this thought that it wasn't like he walked through the woods or was living in them. It was like the woods *imagined* him there or Boobie imagined the *woods* or some shit like that; like Boobie *was* the woods. I started to raise my hand to wave to him, but when I did he disappeared. I woke up feeling all sad and lost.

Seldom went, "Jimster?"

And I was like, "It ain't Scooby, it's Boobie."

"Boobie?"

"Yeah, Boobie."

"Well whatever his name is, it sounded to me like he was in trouble. Like they was chasin' him."

"It don't mean nothin'."

"Sure sounded to me like it meant somethin'."

Seldom bent down and picked up this big long tree branch.

He went, "You was wavin' to him, too."

"I was?"

"Wavin' to him like he was leavin' on a train."

I could still feel that floor from Seldom's bedroom all locked up in my back. I bent down and picked up this little wack stick. I knew Seldom probably wouldn't use it on the raft cuz it was too small, but I picked it up anyway.

Then Seldom picked up another stick and went, "Big Tiny. Scooby. Waving your arms all crazy. You must be having some crazy dreams, Jimster."

I was like, "I must," and threw that little wack stick I picked. I threw that shit far, too.

Then Seldom handed me one of them big sticks he picked and went, "You ever wanna talk about them dreams you keep having, you just let me know, okay?"

But I didn't say nothing back, I just kept looking for sticks.

That's when I decided to skate.

It was like stuff between me and Seldom was getting too wack. He was getting all private investigator pig on me, asking me about my dreams and who was who and what was what and it started to feel like he was trying to *bust* me, like he was one of them Rockdale vagrancy pigs.

So the next morning I told him to go pick sticks without me cuz I wasn't feeling too good — I told him I had ass failure or my toe hurt or some shit and he was like asking me did I need anything, but I told him I was cool.

When he left I put my puffy red coat on and sacked the baby on my back and wrapped that long yellow scarf around my neck and pulled that cinnamon roll hat over my head and stuck them tennis rackets to the bottoms of my Pro Flyers.

Then I made some jelly sandwiches and grabbed a few cans of pinto beans from the cupboard.

When I stuffed them sandwiches and them canned beans in my pockets some wack shit happened. I forgot I had my gat in my pocket. It was like it disappeared for all them weeks I was at the Itty Bitty Farm.

So I was stuffing all that shit in my pockets and I got my fingers all tangled in the trigger, and then — *BLOWWW!* — that shit went off! I shot a hole through all three of them sandwiches and through my pants, and the bullet busted right on through the kitchen floor. And that shit was loud, too!

The baby started crying and my frostbite hand started shaking and you could see a bunch of old skanky dust climbing through the light that was sliding through that hole in the floor.

We skated right after that. You can't just stand

around after your gat goes off. You gotta start running or else them gat pigs will start breaking down the door; even them gat pigs in Nimrod, Minnesota.

At first I thought we should make a run for the forest, but I kept thinking about that dream I had about Boobie and how he just stood there staring at me and how his hair was all white and spooky and shit.

Then I thought about that train whistle and how if we heard it I could just follow it to where the tracks was and make a jump for it, but then all them pictures of me and the baby starving to death and catching lung frosts started getting all stuck in my head, so we didn't do that, neither.

So what we did was we headed back toward the Crow Wing River where the Skylark was hid.

I figured we could hitchhike somewhere and maybe I could make some money by getting a paper route or some shit, but nothing too serious. I figured we'd need a little money to buy pinto beans and diapers and some food for me every once in a while.

I was walking with those tennis rackets pretty good. All that stick collecting with Seldom gave me lots of practice. I could feel my heart drumming in my chest and my blood pushing through my heart and my breath was smoking out all white and thick and that yellow scarf was all wrapped around my neck and the baby was like steering me by my ears.

When we got over by where the van was, some freaky shit started happening. Instead of walking past it, we went back *inside* of it, right up them little rickety stairs.

It still looked the same as when me and Seldom came and got Curl, with them snowfish on the walls and that frost crawling over everything and them newspapers hanging off the windows all yellow and skanky.

Then I started thinking about Curl and Boobie and how at the end everything got all wack and cold and desperate and about how Curl caught her lung frost and kept talking about that big black turkey and how she spray-painted them snowfish on the walls and how she just kept getting sicker and sicker.

And I thought about Boobie and how he drew that fish on Curl's face and how he disappeared through the snowing trees all backwards and how now the only place I seen him was in dreams where his hair wasn't even the right color and how those dreams was making me feel all sad and lost.

And I started thinking about Seldom picking them sticks and going back to the Itty Bitty Farm and climbing up to the roof with his old creaky bones. And I started thinking about him wondering where me and the baby was and him just sort of figuring that I decided to try and meet up with him to pick sticks.

And then I thought about how I wasn't really doing that, how I wasn't picking *shit,* and how I was just running again, and how my whole wack life felt all skanky, and for some reason that made me think of the Christmas tree laying in the backyard and how the popcorn was still on it and them flames sawing in the fireplace and how sometimes when they're tall enough they saw in the window so there's double-sawing, and I even pictured Deuce and her little hooker walk and how I kinda liked watching her coming into the house on her own like she had them special powers.

And then I thought of that little picture of Seldom and his wife on that box next to his bed and how it was so old and yellow in the corners and I thought of that wack little baby crib in the other room and how all them old coats was stacked in it like it didn't mean nothing no more and I thought of that picture of the clown with the balloons in his cheeks and all of that shit was spinning around in my head like a bunch of bees.

Then I practically ran through the van and down them rickety steps and as soon as I got outside I fell to my knees and started doing the second-wackest shit I'll probably ever do in my life:

I started picking up sticks. And I picked about skeighty-eight of them joints. I couldn't even control my hands. I didn't even feel the baby on my back or all that snow sliding through the hole in my pants that that bullet made. I just picked sticks all the way back to the Itty Bitty Farm and I picked them till my hands was raw.

What's funny is that when I got back to the house, Seldom *was* on the roof just like I thought and he *was* joining the new sticks to the raft, and when he saw me and the baby walking through the snow and how my arms was all full of sticks he *was* waving, and he *was* standing up all lopsided and crooked and he *did* almost fall off the roof. He even had to grab onto the chimney.

When he got balanced he put his big old hands up to his face and shouted, "I was wonderin' where you two was."

The sky behind him was turning purple.

Through the living room window you could see the fire going and the light was all yellow and warm-looking.

I put my sticks down and headed inside with the baby.